The Misfortunes of Elphin

Thomas Love Peacock

CONTENTS

INDEX TO THE POETRY

CHAPTER I
The Prosperity of Gwaelod

Regardless of the sweeping whirlwind's sway,
That, hush'd in grim repose, expects his evening prey.
—Gray [*The Bard*, II. 2. 75 f.]

IN THE beginning of the sixth century, when Uther Pendragon held the nominal sovereignty of Britain over a number of petty kings, Gwythno Garanhir was king of Caredigion. The most valuable portion of his dominions was the Great Plain of Gwaelod, an extensive tract of level land, stretching along that part of the sea-coast which now belongs to the counties of Merioneth and Cardigan. This district was populous and highly cultivated. It contained sixteen fortified towns, superior to all the towns and cities of the Cymry, excepting Caer Lleon upon Usk; and, like Caer Lleon, they bore in their architecture, their language, and their manners, vestiges of past intercourse with the Roman lords of the world. It contained also one of the three privileged ports of the isle of Britain, which was called the Port of Gwythno. This port, we may believe if we please, had not been unknown to the Phoenicians and Carthaginians, when they visited the island for metal, accommodating the inhabitants, in return, with luxuries which they would not otherwise have dreamed of, and which they could very well have done without; of course, in arranging the exchange of what they denominated equivalents, imposing on their simplicity, and taking advantage of their ignorance, according to the approved practice of civilized nations; which they called imparting the blessings of Phoenician and Carthaginian light.

An embankment of massy stone protected this lowland country from the sea, which was said, in traditions older than the embankment, to have, in occasional spring-tides, paid short but unwelcome visits to the interior inhabitants, and to have, by slow aggressions, encroached considerably on the land. To prevent the repetition of the first of these inconveniences, and to check the progress of the second, the people of Gwaelod had built the stony rampart, which had withstood the shock of the waves for centuries, when Gwythno began his reign.

Gwythno, like other kings, found the business of governing too light a matter to fill up the vacancy of either his time or his head, and took to the more solid pursuits of harping and singing; not forgetting feasting, in which he was glorious; nor hunting, wherein he was mighty. His several pursuits composed a very harmonious triad. The chace conduced to the good cheer of the feast, and to the good appetite which consumed it; the feast inspired the song; and the song gladdened the feast, and celebrated the chace.

Gwythno and his subjects went on together very happily. They had little to do with him but to pay him revenue, and he had little to do with them but to receive it. Now and then they were called on to fight for the protection of his sacred person, and for the privelege of paying revenue to him rather than to any of the kings in his vicinity, a privilege of which they were particularly tenacious. His lands being far more fertile, and his people, consequently, far more numerous, than those of the rocky dwellers on his borders, he was always victorious in the defensive warfare to which he restricted his military achievements; and, after the invaders of his dominions had received two or three inflictions of signal chastisement, they limited their aggressions to coming quietly in the night, and vanishing, before morning, with cattle: an heroic operation, in which the pre-eminent glory of Scotland renders the similar exploits of other nations not worth recording.

Gwythno was not fond of the sea: a moonstruck bard had warned him to beware of the oppression of Gwenhidwy; and he thought he could best do so by keeping as far as possible out of her way. He had a palace built of choice slate stone on the rocky banks of the Mawddach, just above the point where it quitted its native mountains, and entered the Plain of Gwaelod. Here, among green woods and sparkling waters, he lived in festal munificence, and expended his revenue in encouraging agriculture, by consuming a large quantity of produce.

Watchtowers were erected along the embankment, and watchmen were appointed to guard against the first approaches of damage or decay. The whole of these towers, and their companies of guards, were subordinate to a central castle, which commanded the sea-port already mentioned, and wherein dwelt Prince Seithenyn ap Seithyn Saidi, who held the office of Arglwyd Gorwarcheidwad yr Argae Breninawl, which signifies, in English, Lord High Commissioner of Royal Embankment; and he executed it as a personage so denominated might be expected to do: he drank the profits, and left the embankment to his deputies, who left it to their assistants, who left it to itself.

The condition of the head, in a composite as in a simple body, affects the entire organization to the extremity of the tail, excepting that, as the tail in the figurative body usually receives the largest share in the distribution of punishment, and the smallest in the distribution of reward, it has the stronger stimulus to ward off evil, and the smaller supply of means to indulge in diversion; and it sometimes happens that one of the least regarded of the component parts of the said tail will, from a pure sense of duty, or an inveterate love of business, or an oppressive sense of ennui, or a development of the organ of order, or some other equally cogent reason, cheerfully undergo all the care and labour, of which the honour and profit will redound to higher quarters.

Such a component portion of the Gwaelod High Commission of Royal Embankment was Teithrin ap Tathral, who had the charge of a watchtower where the embankment terminated at the point of Mochres, in the high land of Ardudwy. Teithrin kept his portion of the embankment in exemplary condition, and paced with daily care the limits of his charge; but one day, by some accident, he strayed beyond them, and observed symtoms of neglect that filled him with dismay. This circumstance induced him to proceed till his wanderings brought him round to the embankment's southern termination in the high land of Caredigion. He met with abundant hospitality at the towers of his colleagues, and at the castle of Seithenyn: he was supposed to be walking for his amusement; he was asked no questions, and he carefully abstained from asking any.

The Misfortunes of Elphin

He examined and observed in silence; and, when he had completed his observations, he hastened to the palace of Gwythno.

Preparations were making for a high festival, and Gwythno was composing an ode. Teithrin knew better than to interupt him in his *awen*.

Gwythno had a son named Elphin, who is celebrated in history as the most expert of fishers. Teithrin, finding the king impracticable, went in search of the young prince.

Elphin had been all the morning fishing in the Mawddach, in a spot where the river, having quitted the mountians and not yet entered the plain, ran in alternate streams and pools sparkling through a pastoral valley. Elphin sat under an ancient ash, enjoying the calm brightness of an autumnal noon, and the melody and beauty of the flying stream, on which the shifting sunbeams fell chequering through the leaves. The monotonous music of the river, and the profound stillness of the air, had contributed to the deep abstraction of a meditation into which Elphin had fallen. He was startled into attention by a sudden rush of the wind through the trees, and during the brief interval of transition from the state of reverie to that of perfect consciousness, he heard, or seemed to hear, in the gust that hurried by him, the repetition of the words, "Beware of the oppression of Gwenhidwy." The gust was momentary: the leaves ceased to rustle, and the deep silence of nature returned.

The prophecy, which had long haunted the memory and imagination of his father, had been often repeated to Elphin, and had sometimes occupied his thoughts, but it had formed no part of his recent meditation, and he could not persuade himself that the words had not been actually spoken near him. He emerged from the shade of the trees that fringed the river, and looked round him from the rocky bank.

At this moment Teithrin ap Tathral discovered and approached him.

Elphin knew him not, and inquired his name. He answered, "Teithrin ap Tathral."

"And what seek you here?" said Elphin.

"I seek," answered Teithrin, "the Prince of Gwaelod, Elphin ap Gwythno Garanhir."

"You spoke," said Elphin, "as you approached." Teithrin answered in the negative.

"Assuredly you did," said Elphin. "You repeated the words, "Beware of the oppression of Gwenhidwy.""

Teithrin denied having spoken the words; but their mysterious impression made Elphin listen readily to his information and advice; and the result of their conference was a determination, on the part of the Prince, to accompany Teithrin ap Tathral on a visit of remonstrance to the Lord High Commissioner.

They crossed the centre of the enclosed country to the privileged port of Gwythno, near which stood the castle of Seithenyn. They walked towards the castle along a portion of the embankment, and Teithrin pointed out to the Prince its dilapidated condition. The sea shone with the glory of the setting sun; the air was calm; and the white surf, tinged with the crimson of sunset, broke lightly on the sands below. Elphin turned his eyes from the dazzling splendour of ocean to the green meadows of the Plain of Gwaelod; the trees, that in the distance thickened into woods; the wreaths of smoke rising from am ong them, marking the solitary cottages, or the populous towns; the massy barrier of mountains beyond, with the forest rising from their base; the precipices frowning over the forest; and the clouds resting on their summits, reddened with the reflection of the west. Elphin gazed earnestly on the peopled plain, reposing in the calm of evening between the mountains and the sea, and thought, with deep feelings of secret pain, how much of life and human happiness was intrusted to the ruinous mound on which he stood.

CHAPTER II
The Drunkeness of Seithenyn

The three immortal drunkards of the isle of Britain: Ceraint of Essyllwg; Gwrtheyrn Gwrthenau; and Seithenyn ap Seithyn Saidi. —*Triads of the Isle of Britain.*

THE SUN had sunk beneath the waves when they reached the castle of Seithenyn. The sound of the harp and the song saluted them as they approached it. As they entered the great hall, which was already blazing with the torchlight, they found his highness, and his highness's household, convincing themselves and each other with wine and wassail, of the excellence of their system of virtual superintendence; and the following jovial chorus broke on the ears of the visitors:

THE CIRCLING OF THE MEAD-HORNS

Fill the blue horn, the blue buffalo horn:
Natural is mead in the buffalo horn:
As the cuckoo in spring, as the lark in the morn,
So natural is mead in the buffalo horn.

As the cup of the flower to the bee when he sips,
Is the full cup of mead to the true Briton's lips:
From the flower-cups of summer, on field and on tree,
Our mead cups are filled by the vintager bee.

Seithenyn ap Seithyn, the generous, the bold,
Drinks the wine of the stranger from vessels of gold;
But we from the horn, the blue silver-rimmed horn,
Drink the ale and the mead in our fields that were born.

The ale-froth is white, and the mead sparkles bright;
They both smile apart, and with smiles they unite:*
The mead from the flower, and the ale from the corn,
Smile, sparkle, and sing in the buffalo horn.

> The horn, the blue horn, cannot stand on its tip;
> Its path is right on from the hand to the lip:
> Though the bowl and the wine-cup our tables adorn,
> More natural the draught from the buffalo horn.
>
> But Seithenyn ap Seithyn, the generous, the bold,
> Drinks the bright-flowing wine from the far-gleaming gold:
> The wine, in the bowl by his lip that is worn,
> Shall be glorious as mead in the buffalo horn.
>
> The horns circle fast, but their fountains will last,
> As the stream passes ever, and never is past:
> Exhausted so quickly, replenished so soon,
> They wax and they wane like the horns of the moon.
>
> Fill high the blue horn, the blue buffalo horn;
> Fill high the long silver-rimmed buffalo horn:
> While the roof of the hall by our chorus is torn,
> Fill, fill to the brim, the deep silver-rimmed horn.

Elphin and Teithrin stood some time on the floor of the hall before they attracted the attention of Seithenyn, who, during the chorus, was tossing and flourishing his golden goblet. The chorus had scarcely ended when he noticed them, and immediately roared aloud, "You are welcome all four."

Elphin answered, "We thank you: we are but two."

"Two or four," said Seithenyn, "all is one. You are welcome all. When a stranger enters, the custom in other places is to begin by washing his feet. My custom is, to begin by washing his throat. Seithenyn ap Seithyn Saidi bids you welcome."

Elphin, taking the wine-cup, answered, "Elphin ap Gwythno Garanhir thanks you."

Seithenyn started up. He endeavoured to straighten himself into perpendicularity, and to stand steadily on his legs. He accomplished half his object by stiffening all his joints but those of his ancles, and from these the rest of his body vibrated upwards with the inflexibility of a bar. After thus oscillating for a time, like an inverted pendulum, finding that the attention requisite to preserve his rigidity absorbed all he could collect of his dissipated energies, and that he required a portion of them for the management of his voice, which he felt a dizzy desire to wield with peculiar steadiness in the presence of the son of the king, he suddenly relaxed the muscles that perform the operation of sitting, and dropped into his chair like a plummet. He then, with a gracious gesticulation, invited Prince Elphin to take his seat on his right hand, and proceeded to compose himself into a dignified attitude, throwing his body back into the left corner of his chair, resting his left elbow on its arm and his left cheekbone on the middle of the back of his left hand, placing his left foot on a footstool, and stretching out his right leg as straight and as far as his position allowed. He had thus his right hand at liberty, for the ornament of his eloquence and the conduct of his liquor.

Elphin seated himself at the right hand of Seithenyn. Theithrin remained at the end of the hall: on which Seithenyn exclaimed, "Come on, man, come on. What, if you be not the son of a king, you are the guest of Seithenyn ap Seithenyn Saidi. The most honourable place to the most honourable guest, and the next most honourable place to the next most honourable guest; the least honourable guest above the most honourable inmate; and, where there are but two guests, be the most honourable who he may, the least honourable of the two is next in honour to the most honourable of the two, because they are no more but two; and, where there are only two, there can be nothing between. Therefore sit, and drink. GWIN O EUR: wine from gold."

Elphin motioned Teithrin to approach, and sit next to him.

Prince Seithenyn, whose liquor was "his eating and his drinking solely",* seemed to measure the gastronomy of his guests by his own; but his groom of the pantry thought the strangers might be disposed to eat, and placed before them a choice of provision, on which Teithrin ap Tathral did vigorous execution.

"I pray your excuses," said Seithenyn, "my stomach is weak, and I am subject to dizziness in the head, and my memory is not so good as it was, and my faculties of attention are somewhat impaired, and I would dilate more upon the topic, whereby you should hold me excused, but I am troubled with a feverishness and parching of the mouth, that very much injures my speech, and impedes my saying all I would say, and will say before I have done, in token of my loyalty and fealty to your highness and your highness's house. I must just moisten my lips, and I will then proceed with my observations. Cupbearer, fill.

"Prince Seithenyn," said Elphin, "I have visited you on a subject of deep moment. Reports have been brought to me, that the embankment, which has been so long intrusted to your care, is in a state of dangerous decay."

"Decay," said Seithenyn, "is one thing, and danger is another. Every thing that is old must decay. That the embankment is old, I am free to confess; that it is somewhat rotten in parts, I will not altogether deny; that it is any the worse for that, I do most sturdily gainsay. It does its business well: it works well: it keeps out the water from the land, and it lets in the wine upon the High Commission of Embankment. Cupbearer, fill. Our ancestors were wiser than we: they built it in their wisdom; and, if we should be so rash as to try to mend it, we should only mar it."

"The stonework," said Teithrin, "is sapped and mined: the piles are rotten, broken, and dislocated: the floodgates and sluices are leaky and creaky."

"That is the beauty of it," said Seithenyn. "Some parts of it are rotten, and some parts of it are sound."

"It is well," said Elphin, "that some parts are sound: it were better that all were so."

"So I have heard some people say before," said Seithenyn; "perverse people, blind to venerable antiquity: that very unamiable sort of people, who are in the habit of indulging their reason. But I say, the parts that are rotten give elasticity to those that are sound: they give them elasticity, elasticity, elasticity. If it were all sound, it would break by its own obstinate stiffness: the soundness is checked by the rottenness, and the stiffness is balanced by the elasticity. There is nothing so dangerous as innovation. See the waves in the equinoctial storms, dashing and clashing, roaring and pouring, spattering and battering, rattling and battling against it. I would not be so presumptuous as to say, I could build any thing that would stand against them half an hour; and here this immortal old work, which God forbid the finger of modern mason should bring into jeopardy, this immortal work has stood for centuries, and will stand for centuries more, if we let it alone. It is well: it works well: let well alone. Cupbearer, fill. It was half rotten when I was born, and that is a conclusive reason why it should be three parts rotten when I die."

The whole body of the High Commission roared approbation.

"And after all," said Seithenyn, "the worst that could happen would be the overflow of a springtide, for that was the worst that happened before the embankment was thought of; and, if the high water should come in, as it did before, the low water would go out again, as it did before. We should be no deeper in it than our ancestors were, and we could mend as easily as they could make."

"The level of the sea," said Teithrin, "is materially altered."

"The level of the sea!" exclaimed Seithenyn. "Who ever heard of such a thing as altering the level of the sea? Alter the level of that bowl of wine before you, in which, as I sit here, I see a very ugly reflection of your very goodlooking face. Alter the level of that: drink up the reflection: let me see the face without the reflection, and leave the sea to level itself."

"Not to level the embankment," said Teithrin.

"Good, very good," said Seithenyn. "I love a smart saying, though it hits at me. But, whether yours is a smart saying or no, I do not very clearly see; and, whether it hits at me or no, I do not very sensibly feel. But all is one. Cupbearer, fill."

"I think," pursued Seithenyn, looking as intently as he could at Teithrin ap Tathral, "I have seen something very like you before. There was a fellow here the other day very like you: he stayed here some time: he would not talk: he did nothing but drink: he used to drink till he could not stand, and then he went walking about the embankment. I suppose he thought it wanted mending; but he did not say any thing. If he had, I should have told him to embank his own throat, to keep the liquor out of that. That would have posed him: he could not have answered that: he would not have had a word to say for himself after that."

"He must have been a miraculous person," said Teithrin, "to walk when he could not stand."

"All is one for that," said Seithenyn. "Cupbearer, fill."

"Prince Seithenyn," said Elphin, "if I were not aware that wine speaks in the silence of reason, I should be astonished at your strange vindication of your neglect of duty, which I take shame to myself for not having sooner known and remedied. The wise bard has well observed, "Nothing is done without the eye of the king.""

"I am very sorry," said Seithenyn, "that you see things in a wrong light: but we will not quarrel for three reasons: first, because you are the son of the king, and may do and say what you please, without any one having a right to be displeased: second, because I never quarrel with a guest, even if he grows riotous in his cups: third, because there is nothing to quarrel about; and perhaps that is the best reason of the three; or rather the first is the best, because you are the son of the king; and the third is the second, that is, the second best, because there is nothing to quarrel about; and the second is nothing to the purpose, because, though guests will grow riotous in their cups, in spite of my good orderly example, God forbid I should say, that is the case with you. And I completely agree in the truth of your remark, that reason speaks in the silence of wine."

Seithenyn accompanied his speech with a vehement swinging of his right hand: in so doing, at this point, he dropped his cup: a sudden impulse of rash volition, to pick it dexterously up before he resumed his discourse, ruined all his devices for maintaining dignity; in stooping forward from his chair, he lost his balance, and fell prostrate on the floor.

The whole body of the High Commission arose in simultaneous confusion, each zealous to be the foremost in uplifting his fallen chief. In the vehemence of their uprise, they hurled the benches backward and the tables forward; the crash of cups and bowls accompanied their overthrow; and rivulets of liquor ran gurgling through the hall. The household wished to redeem the credit of their leader in the eyes of the Prince; but the only service they could render him was to participate his discomfiture; for Seithenyn, as he was first in dignity, was also, as was fitting, hardest in skull; and that which had impaired his equilibrium had utterly destroyed theirs. Some fell, in the first impulse, with the tables and benches; others were tripped up by the rolling bowls; and the remainder fell at different points of progression, by jostling against each other, or stumbling over those who had fallen before them.

CHAPTER III
The Oppression of Gwenhidwy

Nid meddw y dyn a allo
Cwnu ei hun a rhodio,
Ac yved rhagor ddiawd:
Nid yw hyny yn veddwdawd.

Not drunk is he, who from the floor
Can rise alone, and still drink more;
But drunk is he, who prostrate lies,
Without the power to drink or rise.

A SIDE door, at the upper end of the hall, to the left of Seithenyn's chair, opened, and a beautiful young girl entered the hall, with her domestic bard, and her attendant maidens.

It was Angharad, the daughter of Seithenyn. The tumult had drawn her from the solitude of her chamber, apprehensive that some evil might befall her father in that incapability of self-protection to which he made a point of bringing himself by set of sun. She gracefully saluted Prince Elphin, and directed the cupbearers, (who were bound, by their office, to remain half sober till the rest of the company were finished off, after which they indemnified themselves at leisure,) she directed the cupbearers to lift up Prince Seithenyn, and bear him from the hall. The cupbearers reeled off with their lord, who had already fallen asleep, and who now began to play them a pleasant march with his nose, to inspirit their progression.

Elphin gazed with delight on the beautiful apparition, whose gentle and serious loveliness contrasted so strikingly with the broken trophies and fallen heroes of revelry that lay scattered at her feet.

"Stranger," she said, "this seems an unfitting place for you: let me conduct you where you will be more agreeably lodged."

"Still less should I deem it fitting for you, fair maiden," said Elphin.

She answered, "The pleasure of her father is the duty of Angharad."

Elphin was desirous to protract the conversation, and this very desire took from him the power of speaking to the purpose. He paused for a moment to collect his ideas, and Angharad stood still, in apparent expectation that he would show symptoms of following, in compliance with her invitation.

In this interval of silence, he heard the loud dashing of the sea, and the blustering of the wind through the apertures of the walls.

This supplied him with what has been, since Britain was Britain, the alpha and omega of British conversation. He said, "It seems a stormy night."

She answered, "We are used to storms: we are far from the mountains, between the lowlands and the sea, and the winds blow round us from all quarters."

There was another pause of deep silence. The noise of the sea was louder, and the gusts pealed like thunder through the apertures. Amidst the fallen and sleeping revellers, the confused and littered hall, the low and wavering torches, Angharad, lovely always, shone with single and surpassing loveliness. The gust died away in murmurs, and swelled again into thunder, and died away in murmurs again; and, as it died away, mixed with the murmurs of the ocean, a voice, that seemed one of the many voices of the wind, pronounced the ominous words, "Beware of the oppression of Gwenhidwy."

They looked at each other, as if questioning whether all had heard alike.

"Did you not hear a voice?" said Angharad, after a pause.

"The same," said Elphin, "which has once before seemed to say to me, 'Beware of the oppression of Gwenhidwy.' "

Teithrin hurried forth on the rampart: Angharad turned pale, and leaned against a pillar of the hall. Elphin was amazed and awed, absorbed as his feelings were in her. The sleepers on the floor made an uneasy movement, and uttered an inarticulate cry.

Teithrin returned. "What saw you?" said Elphin.

Teithrin answered, "A tempest is coming from the west. The moon has waned three days, and is half hidden in clouds, just visible above the mountains: the bank of clouds is black in the west; the scud is flying before them; and the white waves are rolling to the shore."

"This is the highest of the springtides," said Angharad, "and they are very terrible in the storms from the west, when the spray flies over the embankment, and the breakers shake the tower which has its foot in the surf."

"Whence was the voice," said Elphin, "which we heard erewhile? Was it the cry of a sleeper in his drink, or an error of the fancy, or a warning voice from the elements?"

"It was surely nothing earthly," said Angharad, "nor was it an error of the fancy, for we all heard the words, "Beware of the oppression of Gwenhidwy." Often and often, in the storms of the springtides, have I feared to see her roll her power over the fields of Gwaelod."

"Pray heaven she do not tonight," said Teithrin.

"Can there be such a danger?" said Elphin.

"I think," said Teitherin, "of the decay I have seen, and I fear the voice I have heard."

A long pause of deep silence ensued, during which they heard the intermitting peals of the wind, and the increasing sound of the rising sea, swelling progressively into wilder and more menacing tumult, till, with one terrific impulse, the whole violence of the equinoctial tempest seemed to burst upon the shore. It was one of those tempests which occur once in several centuries, and which, by their extensive devastations, are chronicled to eternity; for a storm that signalizes its course with extraordinary destruction, becomes as worthy of celebration as a hero for the same reason. The old bard seemed to be of this opinion; for the turmoil which appalled Elphin, and terrified Angharad, fell upon his ears as the sound of inspiration: the awen came upon him; and, seizing his harp, he mingled his voice and his music with the uproar of the elements:

THE SONG OF THE FOUR WINDS *

Wind from the north: the young spring day
Is pleasant on the sunny mead;
Tho' merry harps at evening play;
The dance gay youths and maidens lead:
The thrush makes chorus from the thorn:
The mighty drinker fills his horn.

Wind from the east: the shore is still;
The mountain-clouds fly tow'rds the sea;
The ice is on the winter-rill;
The great hall fire is blazing free:
The prince's circling feast is spread:
Drink fills with fumes the brainless head.

Wind from the south: in summer shade
'Tis sweet to hear the loud harp ring;
Sweet is the step of comely maid,
Who to the bard a cup doth bring:
The black crow flies where carrion lies:
Where pignuts lurk, the swine will work.

Wind from the west: the autumnal deep
Rolls on the shore its billowy pride:
He, who the rampart's watch must keep,
Will mark with awe the rising tide:
The high springtide, that bursts its mound,
May roll o'er miles of level ground.

Wind from the west: the mighty wave
Of ocean bounds o'er rock and sand;
The foaming surges roar and rave
Against the bulwarks of the land:
When waves are rough, and winds are high,
Good is the land that's high and dry.
Wind from the west: the storm-clouds rise;
The breakers rave; the whirlblasts roar;
The mingled rage of the seas and skies
Bursts on the low and lonely shore:
When safety's far, and danger nigh,
Swift feet the readiest aid supply.

Wind from the west—-

His song was cut short by a tremendous crash. The tower, which had its foot in the sea, had long been sapped by the waves; the storm had prematurely perfected the operation, and the tower fell into the surf, carrying with it a portion of the wall of the main building, and revealing, through the chasm, the white raging of the breakers beneath the blackness of the midnight storm. The wind rushed into the hall, extinguishing the torches within the line of its course, tossing the grey locks and loose mantle of the bard, and the light white drapery and long black tresses of Angharad. With the crash of the falling tower, and the simultaneous shriek of the women, the sleepers started from the floor, staring with drunken amazement; and, shortly after, reeling like an Indian from the wine-rolling Hydaspes, in staggered Seithenyn ap Seithyn.

Seithenyn leaned against a pillar, and stared at the sea through the rifted wall, with wild and vacant surprise. He perceived that there was an innovation, and he felt that he was injured: how, or by whom, he did not quite so clearly discern. He looked at Elphin and Teithrin, at his daughter, and at the members of his household, with a long and dismal aspect of blank and mute interrogation, modified by the struggling consciousness of puzzled self-importance, which seemed to require from his chiefship some word of command in this incomprehensible emergency. But the longer he looked, the less clearly he saw; and the longer he pondered, the less he understood. He felt the rush of the wind; he saw the white foam of the sea; his ears were dizzy with their mingled roar. He remained at length motionless, leaning against the pillar, and gazing on the breakers with fixed and glaring vacancy.

"The sleepers of Gwaelod," said Elphin, "they who sleep in peace and security, trusting to the vigilance of Seithenyn, what will become of them?"

"Warn them with the beacon fire," said Teithrin, "if there be fuel on the summit of the landward tower."

"That of course has been neglected too," said Elphin.

"Not so," said Angharad, "that has been my charge."

Teithrin seized a torch, and ascended the eastern tower, and, in a few minutes, the party in the hall beheld the breakers reddening with the reflected fire, and deeper and yet deeper crimson tinging the whirling foam, and sheeting the massy darkness of the bursting waves.

Seithenyn turned his eyes on Elphin. His recollection of him was extremely faint, and the longer he looked on him he remembered him the less. He was conscious of the presence of strangers, and of the occurrence of some signal mischief, and associated the two circumstances in his dizzy perceptions with a confused but close connexion. He said at length, looking sternly at Elphin, "I do not know what right the wind has to blow upon me here; nor what business the sea has to show itself here; nor what business you have here: but one thing is very evident, that either my castle or the sea is on fire; and I shall be glad to know who has done it, for terrible shall be the vengeance of Seithenyn ap Seithyn. Show me the enemy," he pursued, drawing his sword furiously, and flourishing it over his head, "Show me the enemy; show me the enemy."

An unusual tumult mingled with the roar of the waves; a sound, the same in kind, but greater in degree, with that produced by the loose stones of the beach, which are rolled to and fro by the surf.

Teithrin rushed into the hall, exclaiming, "All is over! the mound is broken; and the springtide is rolling through the breach."

Another portion of the castle wall fell into the mining waves, and, by the dim and thickly-clouded moonlight, and the red blaze of the beacon fire, they beheld a torrent pouring in from the sea upon the plain, and rushing immediately beneath the castle walls, which, as well as the points of the embankment that formed the sides of the breach, continued to crumble away into the waters.

"Who has done this?" vociferated Seithenyn, "Show me the enemy."

"There is no enemy but the sea," said Elphin, "to which you, in y our drunken madness, have abandoned the land. Think, if you can think, of what is passing in the plain. The storm drowns the cries of your victims; but the curses of the perishing are upon you."

"Show me the enemy," vociferated Seithenyn, flourishing his sword more furiously.

Angharad looked deprecatingly at Elphin, who abstained from further reply.

"There is no enemy but the sea," said Teithrin, "against which your sword avails not."

"Who dares to say so?" said Seithenyn. "Who dares to say that there is an enemy on earth against whom the sword of Seithenyn ap Scithyn is unavailing? Thus, thus I prove the falsehood."

And, springing suddenly forward, he leaped into the torrent, flourishing his sword as he descended.

"Oh, my unhappy father!" sobbed Angharad, veiling her face with her arm on the shoulder of one of her female attendants, whom Elphin dexterously put aside, and substituted himself as the supporter of the desolate beauty.

"We must quit the castle," said Teithrin, "or we shall be buried in its ruins. We have but one path of safety, along the summit of the embankment, if there be not another breach between us and the high land, and if we can keep our footing in this hurricane. But there is no alternative. The walls are melting away like snow."

The bard, who was now recovered from his awen, and beginning to be perfectly alive to his own personal safety, conscious at the same time that the first duty of his privileged order was to animate the less-gifted multitude by examples of right conduct in trying emergencies, was the first to profit by Teithrin's admonition, and to make the best of his way through the door that opened to the embankment, on which he had no sooner set his foot than he was blown down by the wind, his harp-strings ringing as he fell. He was indebted to the impediment of his harp, for not being rolled down the mound into the waters which were rising within.

Teithrin picked him up, and admonished him to abandon his harp to its fate, and fortify his steps with a spear. The bard murmured objections: and even the reflection that he could more easily get another harp than another life, did not reconcile him to parting with his beloved companion. He got over the difficulty by slinging his harp, cumbrous as it was, to his left side, and taking a spear in his right hand.

Angharad, recovering from the first shock of Seithenyn's catastrophe, became awake to the imminent danger. The spirit of the Cymric female, vigilant and energetic in peril, disposed her and her attendant maidens to use their best exertions for their own preservation. Following the advice and example of Elphin and Teithrin, they armed themselves with spears, which they took down from the walls.

Teithrin led the way, striking the point of his spear firmly into the earth, and leaning from it on the wind: Angharad followed in the same manner: Elphin followed Angharad, looking as earnestly to her safety as was compatible with moderate care of his own: the attendant maidens followed Elphin; and the bard, whom the result of his first experiment had rendered unambitious of the van, followed the female train. Behind them went the cupbearers, whom the accident of sobriety had qualified to march: and behind them reeled and roared those of the bacchanal rout who were able and willing to move; those more especially who had wives or daughters to support their tottering steps. Some were incapable of locomotion, and others, in the heroic madness of liquor, sat down to await their destiny, as they finished the half-drained vessels.

The bard, who had somewhat of a picturesque eye, could not help sparing a little leisure from the care of his body, to observe the effects before him: the volumed blackness of the storm; the white bursting of the breakers in the faint and scarcely-perceptible moonlight; the rushing and rising of the waters within the mound; the long floating hair and waving drapery of the young women; the red light of the beacon fire falling on them from behind; the surf rolling up the side of the embankment, and breaking almost at their feet; the spray flying above their heads; and the resolution with which they impinged the stony ground with their spears, and bore themselves up against the wind.

Thus they began their march. They had not proceeded far, when the tide began to recede, the wind to abate somewhat of its violence, and the moon to look on them at intervals through the rifted clouds, disclosing the desolation of the inundated plain, silvering the tumultuous surf, gleaming on the distant mountains, and revealing a lengthened prospect of their solitary path, that lay in its irregular line like a ribbon on the deep.

CHAPTER IV
The Lamentations of Gwythno

Ou pausomai tas Charitas
Mousais sugkatamignus,
Hédistan suzugian.
—Euripides [*Heracles*, 674 ff.]

Not, though grief my ages defaces,
Will I cease, in concert dear,
Blending still the gentle graces
With the muses more severe.

KING Gwythno had feasted joyously, and had sung his new ode to a chosen party of his admiring subjects, amidst their, of course, enthusiastic applause. He heard the storm raging without, as he laid himself down to rest: he thought it a very hard case for those who were out in it, especially on the sea; congratulated himself on his own much more comfortable condition; and went to sleep with a pious reflection on the goodness of Providence to himself.

He was roused from a pleasant dream by a confused and tumultuous dissonance, that mingled with the roar of the tempest. Rising with much reluctance, and looking forth from his window, he beheld in the moonlight a half-naked multitude, larger than his palace thrice multiplied could have contained, pressing round the gates, and clamouring for admission and shelter; while beyond them his eye fell on the phænomenon of stormy waters, rolling in the place of the fertile fields from which he derived his revenue.

Gwythno, though a king and his own laureate, was not without sympathy for the people who had the honour and happiness of victualling his royal house, and he issued forth on his balcony full of perplexities and alarms, stunned by the sudden sense of the half-understood calamity, and his head still dizzy from the effects of abruptly-broken sleep, and the vapours of the overnight's glorious festival.

Gwythno was altogether a reasonably good sort of person, and a poet of some note. His people were somewhat proud of him on the latter score, and very fond of him on the former; for even the tenth part of those homely virtues, that decorate the memories of "husbands kind and fathers dear" in every churchyard, are matters of plebeian admiration in the persons of royalty; and every tangible point in every such virtue so located, becomes a convenient peg for the suspension of love and loyalty. While, therefore, they were unanimous in consigning the soul of Seithenyn to a place that no well-bred divine will name to a polite congregation, they overflowed, in the abundance of their own griefs, with a portion of sympathy for Gwythno, and saluted him, as he issued forth on his balcony, with a hearty Duw cadw y Brenin, or God save the King, which he returned with a benevolent wave of the hand; but they followed it up by an intense vociferation for food and lodging, which he received with a pitiful shake of the head.

Meanwhile the morning dawned: the green spots, that peered with the ebbing tide above the waste of waters, only served to indicate the irremediableness of the general desolation.

Gwythno proceeded to hold a conference with his people, as deliberately as the stormy state of the weather and their minds, and the confusion of his own, would permit. The result of the conference was, that they should use their best exertions to catch some stray beeves, which had escaped the inundation, and were lowing about the rocks in search of new pastures. This measure was carried into immediate effect: the victims were killed and roasted, carved, distributed, and eaten, in a very Homeric fashion, and washed down with a large portion of the contents of the royal cellars; after which, having more leisure to dwell on their losses, the fugitives of Gwaelod proceeded to make loud lamentation, all collectively for home and for country, and severally for wife or husband, parent or child, whom the flood had made its victims.

In the midst of these lamentations arrived Elphin and Angharad, with her bard and attendant maidens, and Teithrin ap Tathral. Gwythno, after a consultation, despatched Teithrin and Angharad's domestic bard on an embassy to the court of Uther Pendragon, and to such of the smaller kings as lay in the way, to solicit such relief as their several majesties might be able and willing to afford to a king in distress. It is said, that the bard, finding a royal bardship vacant in a more prosperous court, made the most of himself in the market, and stayed where he was better fed and lodged than he could expect to be in Caredigion; but that Teithrin returned, with many valuable gifts, and most especially one from Merlin, being a hamper, which multiplied an hundredfold by morning whatever was put into it overnight, so that, for a ham and a flask put by in the evening, an hundred hams and an hundred flasks were taken out in the morning. It is at least certain that such a hamper is enumerated among the thirteen wonders of Merlin's art, and, in the authentic catalogue thereof, is called the Hamper of Gwythno. [*]

Be this as it may, Gwythno, though shorn of the beams of his revenue, kept possession of his palace. Elphin married Angharad, and built a salmon-weir on the Mawddach, the produce of which, with that of a series of beehives, of which his princess and her maidens made mead, constituted for some time the principal w ealth and subsistence of the royal family of Caredigion.

King Gwythno, while his son was delving or fishing, and his daughter spinning or making mead, sat all day on the rocks, with his harp between his knees, watching the rolling of ocean over the locality of his past dominion, and pouring forth his soul in pathetic song on the change of his own condition, and the mutability of human things. Two of his songs of lamentation have been preserved by tradition: they are the only relics of his muse which time has spared.

GWYDDNAU EI CANT,

PAN DDOAI Y MOR DROS CANTREV Y GWALAWD.

A SONG OF GWYTHNO GARANHIR,

ON THE INUNDATION OF THE SEA OVER THE PLAIN OF GWAELOD.

Stand forth, Seithenyn: winds are high:
Look down beneath the lowering sky;

The Misfortunes of Elphin

Look from the rock: what meets thy sight?
Nought but the breakers rolling white.

Stand forth, Seithenyn: winds are still:
Look from the rock and heathy hill
For Gwythno's realm: what meets thy view?
Nought but the ocean's desert blue.

Curst be the treacherous mound, that gave
A passage to the mining wave:
Curst be the cup, with mead-froth crowned,
That charmed from thought the trusted mound.

A tumult, and a cry to heaven!
The white surf breaks; the mound is riven:
Through the wide rift the ocean-spring
Bursts with tumultuous ravaging.

The western ocean's stormy might
Is curling o'er the rampart's height:
Destruction strikes with want and scorn
Presumption, from abundance born.

The tumult of the western deep
Is on the winds, affrighting sleep:
It thunders at my chamber-door;
It bids me wake, to sleep no more.

The tumult of the midnight sea
Swells inland, wildly, fearfully:
The mountain-caves respond its shocks
Among the unaccustomed rocks.

The tumult of the vext sea-coast
Rolls inland like an armed host:
It leaves, for flocks and fertile land,
But foaming waves and treacherous sand.

The wild sea rolls where long have been
Glad homes of men, and pastures green:
To arrogance and wealth succeed
Wide ruin and avenging need.

Seithenyn, come: I call in vain:
The high of birth and weak of brain
Sleeps under ocean's lonely roar
Between the rampart and the shore.

The eternal waste of waters, spread
Above his unrespected head,
The blue expanse, with foam besprent,
Is his too glorious monument.

ANOTHER SONG OF GWYTHNO

I love the green and tranquil shore;
I hate the ocean's dizzy roar,
Whose devastating spray has flown
High o'er the monarch's barrier-stone.

Sad was the feast, which he who spread
Is numbered with the inglorious dead;
The feast within the torch-lit hall,
While stormy breakers mined the wall.

To him repentance came too late:
In cups the chatterer met his fate:
Sudden and sad the doom that burst
On him and me, but mine the worst.

I love the shore, and hate the deep:
The wave has robbed my nights of sleep:
The heart of man is cheered by wine;
But now the wine-cup cheers not mine.

The feast, which bounteous hands dispense,

Makes glad the soul, and charms the sense:
But in the circling feast I know
The coming of my deadliest foe.

Blest be the rock, whose foot supplied
A step to them that fled the tide;
The rock of bards, on whose rude steep
I bless the shore, and hate the deep.

"The sigh of Gwythno Garanhir when the breakers ploughed up his land"* is the substance of a proverbial distich, which may still be heard on the coast of Merioneth and Cardigan, to express the sense of an overwhelming calamity. The curious investigator may still land on a portion of the ancient stony rampart; which stretches, off the point of Mochres, far out into Cardigan Bay, nine miles of the summit being left dry, in calm weather, by the low water of the springtides; and which is now called Sarn Badrig, or St. Patrick's Causeway.

Thus the kingdom of Caredigion fell into ruin: its people were destroyed, or turned out of house and home; and its royal family were brought to a condition in which they found it difficult to get loaves to their fishes. We, who live in more enlightened times, amidst the "gigantic strides of intellect," when offices of public trust are so conscientiously and zealously discharged, and so vigilantly checked and superintended, may wonder at the wicked negligence of Seithenyn; at the sophisms with which, in his liquor, he vindicated his system, and pronounced the eulogium of his old dilapidations, and at the blind confidence of Gwythono and his people in this virtual guardian of their lives and property: happy that our own public guardians are too virtuous to act or talk like Seithenyn, and that we ourselves are too wise not to perceive, and too free not to prevent it, if they should be so disposed.

CHAPTER V
The Prize of the Weir

Weave a circle round him thrice,
And close your eyes with holy dread;
For he on honey-dew hath fed,
And drank the milk of paradise.
—Coleridge. [*Kubla Khan*, 51 ff.]

PRINCE Elphin constructed his salmon-weir on the Mawddach at the point where the fresh water met the top of the springtides. He built near it a dwelling for himself and Angharad, for which the old king Gwythno gradually deserted his palace. An amphitheatre of rocky mountains enclosed a pastoral valley. The meadows gave pasture to a few cows; and the flowers of the mountain-heath yielded store of honey to the bees of many hives, which were tended by Angharad and her handmaids. Elphin had also some sheep, which wandered on the mountains. The worst was, they often wandered out of reach; but, when he could not find his sheep, he brought down a wild goat, the venison of Gwyneth. The woods and turbaries supplied unlimited fuel. The straggling cultivators, who had escaped from the desolation of Gwaelod, and settled themselves above the level of the sea, on a few spots propitious to the plough, still acknowledged their royalty, and paid them tribute in corn. But their principal wealth was fish. Elphin was the first Briton who caught fish on a large scale, and salted them for other purposes than home consumption.

The weir was thus constructed: a range of piles crossed the river from shore to shore, slanting upwards from both shores, and meeting at an angle in the middle of the river. A little down the stream a second range of piles crossed the river in the same manner, having towards the middle several wide intervals with light wicker gates, which, meeting at an angle, were held together by the current, but were so constructed as to yield easily to a very light pressure from below. These gates gave all fish of a certain magnitude admission to a chamber, from which they could neither advance nor

28

retreat, and from which, standing on a narrow bridge attached to the lower piles, Elphin bailed them up at leisure. The smaller fish passed freely up and down the river through the interstices of the piles. This weir was put together in the early summer, and taken to pieces and laid by in the autumn.

Prince Elphin, one fine July night, was sleepless and troubled in spirit. His fishery had been beyond all precedent unproductive, and the obstacle which this circumstance opposed to his arrangements for victualling his little garrison kept him for the better half of the night vigilant in unprofitable cogitation. Soon after the turn of midnight, when dreams are true, he was startled from an incipient doze by a sudden cry of Angharad, who had been favored with a vision of a miraculous draught of fish. Elphin, as a drowning man catches at a straw, caught at the shadowy promise of Angharad's dream, and at once, beneath the clear light of the just-waning moon, he sallied forth with his princess to examine his weir.

The weir was built across the stream of the river, just above the flow of the ordinary tides; but the springtide had opened the wicker gates, and had floated up a coracle between a pair of them, which closing, as the tide turned, on the coracle's nose, retained it within the chamber of the weir, at the same time that it kept the gates sufficiently open to permit the escape of any fish that might have entered the chamber. The great prize, which undoubtedly might have been there when Angharad dreamed of it, was gone to a fish.

Elphin, little pleased, stepped on the narrow bridge, and opened the gates with a pole that terminated piscatorially in a hook. The coracle began dropping down the stream. Elphin arrested its course, and guided it to land.

In the coracle lay a sleeping child, clothed in splendid apparel. Angharad took it in her arms. The child opened its eyes, and stretched its little arms towards her with a smile; and she uttered, in delight and wonder at its surpassing beauty, the exclamation of "Taliesin!" "Radiant brow!"

Elphin, nevertheless, looked very dismal on finding no food, and an additional mouth; so dismal, that his physiognomy on that occasion passed into a proverb: "As rueful as Elphin when he found Taliesin."*

In after years, Taliesin, being on the safe side of prophecy, and writing after the event, addressed a poem to Elphin, in the character of the foundling of the coracle, in which he supposes himself, at the moment of his discovery, to have addressed Elphin as follows:

DYHUDDIANT ELFFIN.

THE CONSOLATION OF ELPHIN.

> Lament not, Elphin: do not measure
> By one brief hour thy loss or gain:
> Thy weir tonight has borne a treasure,
> Will more than pay thee years of pain.
> St. Cynllo's aid will not be vain:
> Smooth thy bent brow, and cease to mourn:
> Thy weir will never bear again Such wealth as it tonight has
>   borne.
>
> The stormy seas, the silent rivers,
> The torrents down the steeps that spring,
> Alike of weal or woe are givers,
> As pleases heaven's immortal king.
> Though frail I seem, rich gifts I bring,
> Which in Time's fulness shall appear,
> Greater than if the stream should fling
> Three hundred salmon in thy weir.
>
> Cast off this fruitless sorrow, loading
> With heaviness the unmanly mind:
> Despond not; mourn not; evil boding
> Creates the ill it fears to find.
> When fates are dark, and most unkind
> Are they who most should do thee right,

Then wilt thou know thine eyes were blind
To thy good fortune of tonight.

Though, small and feeble, from my coracle
To thee my helpless hands I spread,
Yet in me breathes a holy oracle
To bid thee lift thy drooping head.
When hostile steps around thee tread,
A spell of power my voice shall wield,
That, more than arms with slaughter red,
Shall be thy refuge and thy shield.

Two years after this event, Angharad presented Elphin with a daughter, whom they named Melanghel. The fishery prospered; and the progress of cultivation and population among the more fertile parts of the mountain districts brought in a little revenue to the old king.

CHAPTER VI
The Education of Taliesin

The three objects of intellect: the true, the beautiful, and the beneficial.

The three foundations of wisdom: youth, to acquire learning; memory, to retain learning; and genius, to illustrate learning. — *Triads of Wisdom.* *

The three primary requisites of poetical genius: an eye, that can see nature; a heart, that can feel nature; and a resolution, that dares follow nature." — *Triads of Poetry.*

AS Taliesin grew up, Gwythno instructed him in all knowledge of the age, which was of course not much, in comparison with ours. The science of political economy was sleeping in the womb of time. The advantage of growing rich by getting into debt and paying interest was altogether unknown: the safe and economical currency, which is produced by a man writing his name on a bit of paper, for which other men give him their property, and which he is always ready to exchange for another bit of paper, of an equally safe and economical manufacture, being also equally ready to render his own person, at a moment's notice, as impalpable as the metal which he promises to pay, is a stretch of wisdom to which the people of those days had nothing to compare. They had no steam-engines, with fires as eternal as those of the nether world, wherein the squalid many, from infancy to age, might be turned into component portions of machinery for the benefit of the purple-faced few. They could neither poison the air with gas, nor the waters with its dregs: in short, they made their money of metal, and breathed pure air, and drank pure water, like unscientific barbarians.

Of moral science they had little; but morals, without science, they had about the same as we have. They had a number of fine precepts, partly from their religion, partly from their bards, which they remembered in their liquor, and forgot in their business.

Political science they had none. The blessings of virtual representation were not even dreamed of; so that, when any of their barbarous metallic currency got into their pockets or coffers, it had a chance to remain there, subjecting them to the inconvenience of unemployed capital. Still they went to work politically much as we do. The powerful took all they could get from their subjects and neighbours; and called something or other sacred and glorious, when they wanted the people to fight for them. They represented disaffection by force, when it showed itself in an overt act; but they encouraged freedom of speech, when it was, like Hamlet's reading, "words, words, words."

There was no liberty of the press, because there was no press; but there was liberty of speech to the bards, whose persons were inviolable, and the general motto of their order was Y GWIR YN ERBYN Y BYD: the Truth against the World. [*] If many of them, instead of acting up to this splendid profession, chose to advance their personal fortunes by appealing to the selfishness, the passions, and the prejudices, of kings, factions, and the rabble, our free press gentry may afford them a little charity out of the excess of their own virtue.

In physical science, they supplied the place of knowledge by converting conjectures into dogmas; an art which is not yet lost. They held that the earth was the centre of the universe; that the immense ocean surrounded the earth; that the sky was a vast frame resting on the ocean; that the circle of their contact was a mystery of infinite mist; with a great deal more of cosmogony and astronomy, equally correct and profound, which answered the same purpose as our more correct and profound astromony answers now, that of elevating the mind, as the eidouranion lecturers have it, to sublime contemplations.

Medicine was cultivated by the Druids, and it was just as much a science with them as with us; but they had not the wit or the means to make it a flourishing trade; the principal means to that end being women with nothing to do, articles which especially belong to a high state of civilization.

The laws lay in a small compass: every bard had those of his own community by heart. The king, or chief, was the judge; the plaintiff and defendant told their own story; and the cause was disposed of in one hearing. We may well boast of the progress of light, when we turn from this picture to the statutes at large, and the Court of Chancery; and we may indulge in a pathetic reflection on our sweet-faced myriads of "learned friends," who would be under the unpleasant necessity of suspending themselves by the neck, if this barbaric "practice of the courts" were suddenly revived.

The religion of the time was Christianity grafted on Druidism. The Christian faith had been very early preached in Britain. Some of the Wel sh historians are of opinion that it was first preached by some of the apostles: most probably by St. John. They think the evidence inconclusive with respect to St. Paul. But, at any rate, the faith had made considerable progress among the Britons at the period of the arrival of Hengist; for many goodly churches, and, what was still better, richly endowed abbeys, were flourishing in many places. The British clergy were, however, very contumacious towards the see of Rome, and would only acknowledge the spiritual authority of the arch-bishopric of Caer Lleon, which was, during many centuries, the primacy of Britain. St. Augustin, when he came over, at a period not long subsequent to that of the present authentic history, to preach Christianity to the Saxons, who had for the most part held fast to their Odinism, had also the secondary purpose of making them instruments for teaching the British clergy submission to Rome: as a means to which end, the newly-converted Saxons set upon the monastery of Bangor Iscoed, and put its twelve hundred monks to the sword. This was the first overt act in which the Saxons set forth their new sense of a religion of peace. It is alleged, indeed, that these twelve hundred monks supported themselves by the labour of their own hands. If they did so, it was, no doubt, a gross heresy; but whether it deserved the castigation it received from St. Augustin's proselytes, may be a question in polemics.

As the people did not read the Bible, and had no religious tracts, their religion, it may be assumed, was not very pure. The rabble of Britons must have seen little more than the superficial facts, that the lands, revenues, privileges, and so forth, which once belonged to Druids and so forth, now belonged to abbots, bishops, and so forth, who, like their extruded precursors, walked occasionally in a row, chanting unintelligible words, and never speaking in common language but to exhort the people to fight; having, indeed, better notions than their predecessors of building, apparel, and cookery; and a better knowledge of the means of obtaining good wine, and of the final purpose for which it was made.

They were observant of all matters of outward form, and tradition even places among them personages who were worthy to have founded a society for the suppression of vice. It is recorded, in the Triads, that "Gwrgi Garwlwyd killed a male and female of the Cymry daily, and devoured them; and, on the Saturday, he killed two of each, that he might not kill on the Sunday." This can only be a type of some sanctimonious hero, who made a cloak of piety for oppressing the poor.

But, even among the Britons, in many of the least populous and most mountainous districts, Druidism was still struggling with Christianity. The lamb had driven the wolf from the rich pastures of the vallies to the high places of the wilderness, where the rites and mysteries of the old religion flourished in secrecy, and where a stray proselyte of the new light was occasionally caught and roasted for the glory of Andraste.

Taliesin, worshipping Nature in her wildest solitudes, often strayed away for days from the dwelling of Elphin, and penetrated the recesses of Eryri, where one especial spot on the banks of Lake Ceirionydd became the favorite haunt of his youth. In these lonely recesses, he became familiar with Druids, who initiated him in their mysteries, which, like all other mysteries, consisted of a quantity of allegorical mummery, pretending to be symbolical of the immortality of the soul, and of its progress through various stages of being; interspersed with a little, too literal, ducking and singeing of the aspirant, by way of trying his mettle, just enough to put him in fear, but not in risk, of his life.

That Taliesin was thoroughly initiated in these mysteries is evident from several of his poems, which have neither head nor tail, and which, having no sense in any other point of view, must necessarily, as a learned mythologist has demonstrated, be assigned to the class of theology, in which an occult sense can be found or made for them, according to the views of the expounder. One of them, a shade less obscure than its companions, unquestionably adumbrates the Druidical doctrine of transmigration. According to this poem, Taliesin had been with the cherubim at the fall of Lucifer, in Paradise at the fall of man, and with Alexander at the fall of Babylon; in the ark with Noah, and in the milky-way with Tetragramaton; and in many other equally marvellous or memorable conditions: showing that, though the names and histories of the new religion were adopted, its doctrines had still to be learned; and, indeed, in all cases of this description, names are changed more readily than doctrines, and doctrines more readily than ceremonies.

When any of the Romans or Saxons, who invaded the island, fell into the hands of the Britons, before the introduction of Christianity, they were handed over to the Druids, who sacrificed them, with pious ceremonies, to their goddess Andraste. These human sacrifices have done much injury to the Druidical character, amongst us, who never practice them in the same way. They lacked, it must be confessed, some of our light, and also some of our prisons. They lacked some of our light, to enable them to perceive that the act of coming, in great multitudes, with fire and sword, to the remote dwellings of peaceable men, with the premeditated design of cutting their throats, ravishing their wives and daughters, killing their children, and appropriating their worldly goods, belongs, not to the department of murder and robbery, but to that of legitimate war, of which all the practitioners are gentlemen, and entitled to be treated like gentlemen. They lacked some of our prisons, in which our philanthropy has provided accoommodation for so large a portion of our own people, wherein, if they had left their prisoners alive, they could have kept them from returning to their countrymen, and being at their old tricks again immediately. They would also, perhaps, have found some difficulty in feeding them, from the lack of the county rates, by which the most sensible and amiable part of our nation, the country squires, contrive to coop up, and feed, at the public charge, all who meddle with the wild animals of which they have given themselves the monopoly. But as the Druids could neither lock up their captives, nor trust them at large, the darkness of their intellect could suggest no alternative to the process they adopted, of putting them out of the way, which they did with all the sanctions of religion and law. If one of these old Druids could have slept, like the seven sleepers of Ephesus, and awaked, in the nineteenth century, some fine morning near Newgate, the exhibition of some half-dozen funipendulous forgers might have shocked the tender bowels of his humanity, as much as one of his wicker baskets of captives in the flames shocked those of Cæsar [*]; and it would, perhaps, have been difficult to convince him that paper credit was not an idol, and one of a more sanguinary character than his Andraste. The Druids had their view of these matters, and we have ours; and it does not comport with the steam-engine speed of our march of mind to look at more than one side of a question.

The people lived in darkness and vassalage. They were lost in the grossness of beef and ale. They had no pamphleteering societies to demonstrate that reading and writing are better than meat and drink; and they were utterly destitute of the blessings of those "schools for all," the house of correction, and the treadmill, wherein the autochthonal justice of our agrestic kakistocracy now castigates the heinous sins which were then committed with impunity, of treading on old foot-paths, picking up dead wood, and moving on the face of the earth within sound of the whirr of a partridge.

The learning of the time was confined to the bards. It consisted in a somewhat complicated art of versification; in a great number of pithy apophthegms, many of which have been handed down to posterity under the title of the Wisdom of Catog; in an interminable accumulation of Triads, in which form they bound up all their knowledge, physical, traditional, and mythological; and in a mighty condensation of mysticism, being the still-cherished relics of the Druidical rites and doctrines.

The Druids were the sacred class of the bardic order. Before the change of religion, it was by far the most numerous class; for the very simple reason, that there was most to be got by it: all ages and nations having been sufficiently enlightened to make the trade of priest more profitable than that of poet. During this period, therefore, it was the only class that must attracted the notice of foreigners. After the change of religion, the denomination was retained as that of the second class of the order. The Bardd Braint, or Bard of Presidency, was the ruling order, and wore a robe of sky-blue. The Derwydd, or Druid, wore a robe of white. The Ovydd, or Ovate, was of the class of initiation, and wore a robe of green. The Awenyddion, or disciples, the candidates for admission into the Bardic order, wore a variegated dress of the three colours, and were passed through a very severe moral and intellectual probation.

Gwythno was a Bardd Braint, or Bard of Presidency, and as such he had full power in his own person, without the intervention of a Bardic Congress, to make his Awenydd or disciple, Taliesin, an Ovydd or Ovate, which he did accordingly. Angharad, under the old king's instructions, prepared the green robe of the young aspirant's investiture. He afterwards acquired the white robe amongst the Druids of Eryri.

In all Bardic learning, Gwythno was profound. All that he knew he taught to Taliesin. The youth drew in the draughts of inspiration among the mountain forests and the mountain streams, and grew up under the roof of Elphin, in the perfection of genius and beauty.

CHAPTER VII
The huntings of Maelgon

Aiei to men zé, to de methistatai kakon,
To d' ekpephéimen autik' ex archés neon.
—Euripides. [fgt. 35, Nauck]

One ill is ever clinging;
One treads upon its heels:
A third in distance springing,
Its fearful front reveals.

GWYTHNO slept, not with his fathers, for they were under the sea, but as near to them as was found convenient, within the sound of the breakers that rolled over their ancient dwellings. Elphin was now king of Caredigion, and was lord of a large but thinly-peopled tract of rock, mountain, forest, and bog. He held his sovereignty, however, not, as Gwythno had done during the days of the glory of Gwaelod, by that most indisputable sort of right which consists in might, but by the more precarious tenure of the absence of inclination in any of his brother kings to take away any thing he had.

Uther Pendragon, like Gwythno, went the way of all flesh, and Arthur reigned in Caer Lleon, as king of the kings of Britain. Maelgon Gwyneth was then king of that part of North Wales which bordered on the kingdom of Caredigion.

Maelgon was a mighty hunter, and roused the echoes of the mountains with horn and with hound. He went forth to the chace as to war, provisioned for day and weeks, and supported by bard and butler, and all the apparel of princely festivity. He pitched his tents in the forest of Snowdon, by the shore of lake or torrent; and, after hunting all the day, he feasted half the night. The light of his torches gleamed on the foam of the cataracts, and the sound of harp and song was mingled with their midnight roar.

When not thus employed, he was either feasting in his castle of Diganwy, on the Conwy, or fighting with any of the neighbouring kings, who had any thing which he wanted, and which he thought himself strong enough to take from them.

Once, towards the close of autumn, he carried the tumult of the chace into the recesses of Meirion. The consonance, or dissonance, of men and dogs, outpealed the noise of the torrents among the rocks and woods of the Mawddach. Elphin and Teithrin were gone after the sheep or goats in the mountains; Taliesin was absent on the borders of his favorite lake; Angharad and Melanghel were alone. The careful mother, alarmed at the unusual din, and knowing, by rumor, of what materials the Nimrods of Britain were made, fled, with her daughter and handmaids, to the refuge of a deeply-secluded cavern, which they had long before noted as a safe retreat from peril. As they ascended the hills that led to the cavern, they looked back, at intervals, through the openings of the woods, to the growing tumult on the opposite side of the valley. The wild goats were first seen, flying in all directions, taking prodigious leaps from crag to crag, now and then facing about, and rearing themselves on their hind legs, as if in act to butt, and immediately thinking better of it, and springing away on all fours among the trees. Next, the more rare spectacle of a noble stag presented itself on the summit of a projecting rock, pausing a moment to snuff the air, then bounding down the most practicable slope to the valley. Next, on the summit which the stag had just deserted, appeared a solitary huntsman, sitting on a prancing horse, and waking a hundred echoes with the blast of his horn. Next rushed into view the main body of the royal company, and the two-legged and four-legged avalanche came thundering down on the track of the flying prey: not without imminent hazard of broken necks; though the mountain-bred horses, which possessed by nature almost the surefootedness of mules, had finished their education under the first professors of the age.

The stag swam the river, and stood at bay before the dwelling of Elphin, where he was in due time despatched by the conjoint valour of dog and man. The royal train burst into the solitary dwelling, where, finding nothing worthy of much note, excepting a large store of salt salmon and mead, they proceeded to broil and tap, and made fearful havoc among the family's winter provision. Elphin and Teithrin, returning to their expected dinner, stood aghast on the threshold of their plundered sanctuary. Maelgon condescended to ask them who they were; and, learning Elphin's name and quality, felt himself bound to return his involuntary hospitality by inviting him to Diganwy. So strong was his sense of justice on this head, that, on Elphin's declining the invitation, which Maelgon ascribed to modesty, he desired two of his grooms to take him up and carry him off.

So Elphin was impressed into royal favor, and was feasted munificently in the castle of Diganwy. Teithrin brought home the ladies from the cavern, and, during the absence of Elphin, looked after the sheep and goats, and did his master's business as well as his own.

One evening, when the royal "nowle" was "tottie of the must," * while the bards of Maelgon were singing the praises of their master, and of all and every thing that belonged to him, as the most eximious and transcendent persons and things of the superficial garniture of the earth, Maelgon said to Elphin, " My bards say that I am the best and bravest of kings, that my queen is the most beautiful and chaste of women, and that they themselves, by virtue of belonging to me, are the best and wisest of bards. Now what say you, on these heads?"

This was a perplexing question to Elphin, who, nevertheless, answered: "That you are the best and bravest of kings I do not in the least doubt; yet I cannot think that any woman surpasses my own wife in beauty and chastity; or that any bard equals my bard in genius and wisdom."

"Hear you him, Rhûn?" said Maelgon.

"I hear," said Rhûn, "and mark."

Rhûn was the son of Maelgon, and a worthy heir apparent of his illustrious sire. Rhûn set out the next morning on an embassy very similar to Tarquin's, * accompanied by only one attendant. They lost their way and each other, among the forests of Meirion. The attendant, after riding about some time in great trepidation, thought he heard the sound of a harp, mixed with the roar of the torrents, and following its indications, came at length within sight of an oak-fringed precipice, on the summit of which stood Taliesin, playing and singing to the winds and waters. The attendant could not approach him without dismounting; therefore, tying his horse to a branch, he ascended the rock, and, addressing the young bard, inquired his way to the dwelling of Elphin. Taliesin, in return, inquired his business there; and, partly by examination, partly by divination, ascertained his master's name, and the purport of his visit.

Taliesin deposited his harp in a dry cavern of the rock, and undertook to be the stranger's guide. The attendant remounted his horse, and Taliesin preceded him on foot. But the way by which he led him grew more and more rugged, till the stranger called out, "Whither lead you, my friend? My horse can no longer keep his footing." "There is no other way," said Taliesin. "But give him to my management, and do you follow on foot." The attendant consented. Taliesin mounted the horse, and presently struck into a more practicable track; and immediately giving the horse the reins, he disappeared among the woods, leaving the unfortunate equerry to follow as he might, with no better guide than the uncertain recollection of the sound of his horse's heels.

Taliesin reached home before the arrival of Rhûn, and warned Angharad of the mischief that was designed her.

Rhûn, arriving at his destination, found only a handmaid dressed as Angharad, and another officiating as her attendant. The fictitious princess gave him a supper, and everything else he asked for; and, at parting in the morning, a lock of her hair, and a ring, which Angharad had placed on her finger.

After riding a short distance on his return, Rhûn met his unlucky attendant, torn, tired, and half-starved, and cursing some villain who had stolen his horse. Rhûn was too happy in his own success to have a grain of sympathy for his miserable follower, whom he left to find his horse and his way, or either, or neither, as he might, and returned alone to Diganwy.

Maelgon exultingly laid before Elphin the proofs of his wife's infidelity. Elphin examined the lock of hair, and listened to the narration of Rhûn. He divined at once the trick that had been put upon the prince; but he contented himself with saying, "I do not believe that Rhûn has received the favors of Angharad; and I still think that no wife in Britain, not even the queen of Maelgon Gwyneth, is more chaste or more beautiful than mine."

Hereupon Maelgon waxed wroth. Elphin, in a point which much concerned him, held a belief of his own, different from that which his superiors in worldly power required him to hold. Therefore Maelgon acted as the possessors of worldly power usually act in similar cases: he locked Elphin up within four stone walls, with an intimation that he should keep him there till he pronounced a more orthodox opinion on the question in dispute.

CHAPTER VIII
The Love of Melanghel

Alla teais palaméisi machémona thurson aeirón,
Aitheros axia rhexon: epei Dios ambrotos aulé
Ou se ponón apaneuthe dedexetai: oude soi Hórai
Mépó aethleusanti pulas petasósin Olumpou.

Grasp the bold thyrsus; seek the field's array;
And do things worthy of ethereal day;
Not without toil to earthborn man befalls
To tread the floors of Jove's immortal halls:
Never to him, who not by deeds has striven,
Will the bright Hours roll back the gates of heaven.
Iris to Bacchus, in the 13th Book
of the *Dionysiaca* of Nonnus.

THE HOUSEHOLD of Elphin was sufficiently improsperous during the absence of its chief. The havoc which Maelgon's visitation had made in their winter provision, it required the utmost exertions of their collective energies to repair. Even the young princess Melanghel sallied forth, in the garb of a huntress, to strike the deer or the wild goat among the wintry forests, on the summits of the bleak crags, or in the vallies of the flooded streams.

Taliesin, on these occasions, laid aside his harp, and the robe of his order, and accompanied the princess with his hunting spear, and more succinctly apparelled.

Their retinue, it may be supposed, was neither very numerous nor royal, nor their dogs very thoroughbred. It sometimes happened that the deer went one way, the dogs another; the attendants, losing sight of both, went a third, leaving Taliesin, who never lost sight of Melanghel, alone with her among the hills.

One day, the ardor of the chace having carried them far beyond their ordinary bounds, they stood alone together on Craig Aderyn, the

Rock of Birds, which overlooks the river Dysyni. This rock takes its name from the flocks of birds which have made it their dwelling, and which make the air resonant with their multitudinous notes. Around, before, and above them, rose mountain beyond mountain, soaring above the leafless forests, to lose their heads in mist; beneath them lay the silent river; and along the opening of its narrow valley, they looked to the not-distant sea.

"Prince Llywarch," said Taliesin, "is a bard and a warrior: he is the son of an illustrious line. Taliesin is neither prince nor warrior: he is the unknown child of the waters."

"Why think you of Llywarch?" said Melanghel, to whom the name of the prince was known only from Taliesin, who knew it only from fame.

"Because," said Taliesin, "there is that in my soul which tells me that I shall have no rival among the bards of Britain: but, if its princes and warriors seek the love of Melanghel, I shall know that I am but a bard, and not as Llywarch."

"You would be Prince Taliesin," said Melanghel, smiling, "to make me your princess. Am I not a princess already? and such an one as is not on earth, for the land of my inheritance is under the sea, under those very waves that now roll within our view; and, in truth, you are as well qualified for a prince as I am for a princess, and have about as valuable a dominion in the mists and the clouds as I have under the waters."

Her eyes sparkled with affectionate playfulness, while her long black hair floated loosely in the breeze that pressed the folds of her drapery against the matchless symmetry of her form.

"Oh, maid!" said Taliesin, "what shall I do to win your love?"

"Restore me my father," said Melanghel, with a seriousness as winning as her playfulness had been fascinating.

"That will I do," said Taliesin, "for his own sake. What shall I do for yours?"

"Nothing more," said Melanghel, and she held out her hand to the youthful bard. Taliesin seized it with rapture, and pressed it to his lips; then, still grasping her hand, throwing his left arm round her, he pressed his lips to hers.

Melanghel started from him, blushing, and looked at him a moment with something like severity; but he blushed as much as she did, and seemed even more alarmed at her displeasure than she was at his momentary audacity. She reassured him with a smile; and, pointing her spear in the direction of her distant home, she bounded before him down the rock.

This was the kiss of Taliesin to the daughter of Elphin, which is celebrated in an inedited triad, as one of "the Three Chaste Kisses of the island of Britain."

CHAPTER IX
The Education of Taliesin

The three objects of intellect: the true, the beautiful, and the beneficial.

Three things that will always swallow, and never be satisfied: the sea; a burial ground; and a king. —*Triads of Wisdom*

THE HALL of Maelgon Gwyneth was ringing with music and revelry, when Taliesin stood on the floor, with his harp, in the midst of the assembly, and, without introduction or preface, struck a few chords, that, as if by magic, suspended all other sounds, and fixed the attention of all in silent expectation. He then sang as follows:

CANU Y MEDD

THE MEAD SONG OF TALIESIN

The King of kings upholds the heaven,
And parts from earth the billowy sea:
By Him all earthly joys are given;
He loves the just, and guards the free.
Round the wide hall, for thine and thee,
With purest draughts the mead-horns foam,
Maelgon of Gwyneth! Can it be
That here a prince bewails his home?

The bee tastes not the sparkling draught
Which mortals from his toils obtain;
That sends, in festal circles quaffed,
Sweet tumult through the heart and brain.
The timid, while the horn they drain,
Grow bold; the happy more rejoice;
The mourner ceases to complain;
The gifted bard exalts his voice.

To royal Elphin life I owe,
Nurture and name, the harp, and mead:
Full, pure, and sparkling be their flow,
The horns to Maelgon's lips decreed:
For him may horn to horn succeed,
Till, glowing with their generous fire,
He bid the captive chief be freed,
Whom at his hands my songs require.

Elphin has given me store of mead,
Mead, ale, and wine, and fish, and corn;
A happy home; a splendid steed,
Which stately trappings well adorn.
Tomorrow be the auspicious morn
That home the expected chief shall lead;
So may King Maelgon drain the horn
In thrice three million feasts of mead.

"I give you," said Maelgon, "all the rights of hospitality, and as many horns as you please of the mead you so well and justly extol. If you be Elphin's bard, it must be confessed he spoke truth with respect to you, for you are a much better bard than any of mine, as they are all free to confess: I give them that liberty."

The bards availed themselves of the royal indulgence, and confessed their own inferiority to Taliesin, as the king had commanded them to do. Whether they were all as well convinced of it as they professed to be, may be left to the decision of that very large class of literary gentlemen who are in the habit of favoring the reading public with their undisguised opinions.

"But," said Maelgon, "your hero of Caredigion indulged himself in a very unjustifiable bravado with respect to his queen; for he said she was as beautiful and as chaste as mine. Now Rhûn has proved the contrary, with small trouble, and brought away trophies of his triumph; yet still Elphin persists in his first assertion, wherein he grossly disparages the queen of Gwyneth; and for this I hold him in bondage, and will do, till he make recantation."

"That he will never do," said Taliesin, "Your son received only the favors of a handmaid, who was willing, by strategem, to preserve her lady from violence. The real Angharad was concealed in a cavern."

Taliesin explained the adventure of Rhûn, and pronounced an eulogium on Angharad, which put the king and prince into a towering passion.

Rhûn secretly determined to set forth on a second quest; and Maelgon swore by his mead-horn he would keep Elphin till doomsday. Taliesin struck his harp again, and, in a tone of deep but subdued feeling, he poured forth the

SONG OF THE WIND *

The winds that wander far and free,
Bring whispers from the shores and they sweep
Voices of feast and revelry;
Murmurs of forests and the deep;

Low sounds of torrents from the steep
Descending on the flooded vale;
And tumults from the leaguered keep,
Where foes the dizzy rampart scale.

The whispers of the wandering wind
Are borne to gifted ears alone;
For them it ranges unconfined,
And speaks in accents of its own.

It tells me of Deheubarth's throne;
The spider weaves not in its shield:*
Already from its towers is blown
The blast that bids the spoiler yield.

Ill with his prey the fox may wend,
When the young lion quits his lair:
Sharp sword, strong shield, stout arm, should tend
On spirits that unjustly dare.

To me the wandering breezes bear
The war-blast from Caer Lleon's brow;
The avenging storm in brooding there
To which Diganwy's towers shall bow.

"If the wind talks to you," said Maelgon, "I may say, with the proverb, you talk to the wind; for I am not to be sung, or cajoled, or vapored, or bullied out of my prisoner. And as to your war-blasts from Caer Lleon, which I construe into a threat that you will stir up King Arthur against me, I can tell you for your satisfaction, and to spare you the trouble of going so far, that he has enough to do with seeking his wife, who has been carried off by some unknown marauder, and with fighting the Saxons, to have much leisure or inclination to quarrel with a true Briton, who is one of his best friends, and his heir presumptive; for, though he is a man of great prowess, and moreover, saving his reverence and your presence, a cuckold, he has not yet favored his kingdom with an heir apparent. And I request you to understand, that when I extolled you above my bards, I did so only in respect of your verse and voice, melody and execution, figure and action, in short, of your manner; for your matter is naught; and I must do my own bards the justice to say, that, however much they may fall short of you in the requisites aforesaid, they know much better than you do, what is fitting for bards to sing, and kings to hear."

The bards, thus encouraged, recovered from the first shock of Maelgon's ready admission of Taliesin's manifest superiority, and struck up a sort of consecutive chorus, in a series of pennillion, or stanzas, in praise of Maelgon and his heirship presumptive, giving him credit for all the virtues of which the reputation was then in fashion; and, amongst the rest, they very loftily celebrated his justice and magnanimity.

Taliesin could not reconcile his notions of these qualities with Maelgon's treatment of Elphin. He changed his measure and his melody, and pronounced, in impassioned numbers, the poem which a learned Welsh historian calls "The Indignation of the Bards," though, as the indignation was Taliesin's, and not theirs, he seems to have made a small mistake in regard to the preposition.

THE INDIGNATION OF TALIESIN

WITH THE BARDS OF MAELGON GWYNETH

False bards the sacred fire pervert,
Whose songs are won without desert;
Who falsehoods weave in specious lays,
To gild the base with virtue's praise.

From court to court, from tower to tower,
In warrior's tent, in lady's bower,
For gold, for wine, for food, for fire,
They tune their throats at all men's hire.

Their harps re-echo wide and far
With sensual love, and bloody war,
And drunkenness, and flattering lies:
Truth's light may shine for other eyes.

In palaces they still are found,
At feasts, promoting senseless sound:
He is their demigod at least,
Whose only virtue is his feast

They love to talk: they hate to think:
All day they sing; all night they drink:
No useful toils their hands employ;
In boisterous throngs is all their joy.

The bird will fly, the fish will swim,
The bee the honied flowers will skim;

Its food by toil each creature brings,
Except false bards and worthless kings.

Learning and wisdom claim to find
Homage and succour from mankind;
But learning's right, and wisdom's due,
Are falsely claimed by slaves like you.

True bards know truth, and truth will show
Ye know it not, nor care to know:
Your king's weak mind false judgment warps;
Rebuke his wrong, or break your harps.

I know the mountain and the plain;
I know where right and justice reign;
I from the tower will Elphin free;
Your king shall learn his doom from me.

A spectre of the marsh shall rise,
With yellow teeth, and hair, and eyes,
From whom your king in vain aloof
Shall crouch beneath the sacred roof.

He through the half-closed door shall spy
The Yellow Spectre sweeping by;
To whom the punishment belongs
Of Maelgon's crimes and Elphin's wrongs.

By the name of the Yellow Spectre, Taliesin designated a pestilence, which afterwards carried off great multitudes of the people, and, amongst them, Maelgon Gwyneth, then sovereign of Britain, who had taken refuge from it in a church.

Maelgon paid little attention to Taliesin's prophecy, but he was much incensed by the general tenor of his song.

"If it were not," said Maelgon, "that I do not choose to add to the number of the crimes of which you so readily accuse me, that of disregarding the inviolability of your bardship, I would send you to keep company with your trout-catching king, and you might amuse his salmon-salting majesty with telling him as much truth as he is disposed to listen to; which, to judge by his reception of Rhûn's story of his wife, I take to be exceedingly little. For the present, you are welcome to depart; and, if you are going to Caer Lleon, you may present my respects to King Arthur, and tell him, I hope he will beat the Saxons, and find his wife; but I hope, also, that the cutting me off with an heir apparent will not be the consequence of his finding her, or (which, by the by, is more likely,) of his having lost her."

Taliesin took his departure from the hall of Diganwy, leaving the bards biting their lips at his rebuke, and Maelgon roaring with laughter at his own very excellent jest.

CHAPTER X
The Disappointment of Rhûn

Parthene, pós metameipsas ereuthaleén seo morphén?
Eiarinén d'aktina tis esbese seio prosópou?
Ouketi són meleón amarussetai arguphos aiglé:
Ouketi d', ós to prosthe, teai geloósin opópai.

Sweet maid, what grief has changed thy roseate grace,
And quenched the vernal sunshine of thy face?
No more thy light form sparkles as it flies,
Nor laughter flashes from thy radiant eyes.
Venus to Pasithea, in the 33rd Book
of the *Dionysiaca* of Nonnus. [29 ff.]

TALIESIN returned to the dwelling of Elphin, auguring that, in consequence of his information, Rhûn would pay it another visit. In this anticipation he was not mistaken, for Rhûn very soon appeared, with a numerous retinue, determined, apparently, to carry his point by force of arms. He found, however, no inmate in the dwelling but Taliesin and Teithrin ap Tathral.

Rhûn stormed, entreated, promised, and menaced, without success. He perlustrated the vicinity, and found various caverns, but not the one he sought. He passed many days in the search, and, finally, departed; but, at a short distance, he dismissed all his retinue, except his bard of all work, or laureate expectant, and, accompanied by this worthy, returned to the banks of Mawddach, where they resolved themselves into an ambuscade. It was not long before they saw Taliesin issue from the dwelling, and begin ascending the hill. They followed him, at a cautious distance; first up a steep ascent of the forest-covered rocks; then along a small space of densely-wooded tableland, to the edge of a dingle; and, again, by a slight descent, to the bed of a mountain stream, in a spot where the torrent flung itself, in a series of cataracts, down the rift of a precipitous rock, that towered high above their heads. About half-way up the rock, near the base of one of these cataracts, was a projecting ledge, or natural platform of rock, behind which was seen the summit of the opening of a cave. Taliesin paused, and looked around him, as if to ascertain that he was unobserved; and then, standing on a projection of the rock below, he mingled, in spontaneous song, the full power of his voice with the roar of the waters.

TALESIN.

Maid of the rock! though loud the flood,
My voice will pierce thy cell:
No foe is in the mountain wood;
No danger in the dell:
The torrents bound along the glade;
Their path is free and bright;
Be thou as they, oh mountain maid!
In liberty and light.

Melanghel appeared on the rocky platform, and answered the song of her lover:

MELANGHEL.

The cataracts thunder down the steep;
The woods all lonely wave:
Within my heart the voice sinks deep
That calls me from my cave.
The voice is dear, the song is sweet,
And true the words must be:
Well pleased I quit the dark retreat,
To wend away with thee.

TALESIN.

Not yet; not yet: let nightdews fall,
And stars be bright above,
Ere to her long deserted hall
I guide my gentle love.
When torchlight flashes on the roof,

No foe will near thee stray:
Even now his parting courser's hoof
Rings from the rocky way.

MELANGHEL.

Yet climb the path, and comfort speak,
To cheer the lonely cave,
Where woods are bare, and rocks are bleak,
And wintry torrents rave.
A dearer home my memory knows,
A home I still deplore;
Where firelight glows, while winds and snows
Assail the guardian door.

Taliesin vanished a moment from the sight of Rhûn, and almost immediately reappeared by the side of Melanghel, who had now been joined by her mother. In a few minutes she returned, and Angharad and Melanghel withdrew.

Rhûn watched him from the dingle, and then proceeded to investigate the path by which he had gained the platform. After some search he discovered it, ascended to the platform, and rushed into the cavern.

They here found a blazing fire, a half-finished dinner, materials of spinning and embroidering, and other signs of female inhabitancy; but they found not the inhabitants. They searched the cavern to its depth, which was not inconsiderable; much marvelling how the ladies had vanished. While thus engaged, they heard a rushing sound, and a crash on the rocks, as of some ponderous body. The mystery of this noise was very soon explained to them, in a manner that gave an unusual length to their faces, and threw a deep tinge of blue into their rosy complexions. A ponderous stone, which had been suspended like a portcullis at the mouth of the cavern, had been dropped by some unseen agency, and made them as close prisoners as Elphin.

They were not long kept in suspense as to how this matter had been managed. The hoarse voice of Teithrin ap Thathral sounded in their ears from without, "Foxes! you have been seen through, and you are fairly trapped. Eat and drink. You shall want nothing but to get out; which you must want some time; for it is sworn that no hand but Elphin's shall raise the stone of your captivity."

"Let me out," vociferated Rhûn, "and on the word of a prince—-" but, before he could finish the sentence, the retreating steps of Teithrin were lost in the roar of the torrent.

CHAPTER XI
The Heroes of the Dinas Vawr

L'ombra sua torna ch'era dipartita. DANTE, [*]

While there is life there is hope. *English Proverb.*

PRINCE Rhûn being safe in schistous bastile, Taliesin commenced his journey to the court of King Arthur. On his way to Caer Lleon, he was received with all hospitality, entertained with all admiration, and dismissed with all honour, at the castles of several petty kings, and, amongst the rest, at the castle of Dinas Vawr, on the Towy, which was then garrisoned by King Melvas, who had marched with a great force out of his own kingdom, on the eastern shores of the Severn, to levy contributions in the country to the westward, where, as the pleasure of his company had been altogether unlooked for, he had got possession of a good portion of moveable property. The castle of Dinas Vawr presenting itself to him as a convenient hold, he had taken it by storm; and having cut the throats of the former occupants, thrown their bodies into the Towy, and caused a mass to be sung for the good of their souls, he was now sitting over his bowl, with the comfort of a good conscience, enjoying the fruits of the skill and courage with which he had planned and accomplished his scheme of ways and means for the year.

The hall of Melvas was full of magnanimous heroes, who were celebrating their own exploits in sundry choruses, especially in that which follows, which is here put upon record as being the quintessence of all the war-songs that ever were written, and the sum and substance of all the appetencies, tendencies, and consequences of military glory:

THE WAR-SONG OF DINAS VAWR

The mountain sheep are sweeter,
But the valley sheep are fatter;
We therefore deemed it meeter

To carry off the latter.
We made an expedition;
We met a host, and quelled it;
We forced a strong position.
And killed the men who held it.

On Dyfed's richest valley,
Where herds of kine were brousing,
We made a mighty sally,
To furnish our carousing.
Fierce warriors rushed to meet us;
We met them, and o'erthrew them;
They struggled hard to beat us;
But we conquered them, and slew them.

As we drove our prize at leisure,
The king marched forth to catch us:
His rage surpassed all measure,
But his people could not match us.
He fled to his hall-pillars;
And, ere our force we led off,
Some sacked his house and cellars,
While others cut his head off.

We there, in strife bewild'ring,
Split blood enough to swim in:
We orphaned many children,
And widowed many women.
The eagles and the ravens
We glutted with our foemen;
The heroes and the cravens,
The spearmen and the bowmen.

We brought away from battle,
And much their land bemoaned them,
Two thousand head of cattle,
And the head of him who owned them:
Ednyfed, king of Dyfed,

His head was borne before us;
His wine and beasts supplied our feasts,
And his overthrow, our chorus.

As the doughty followers of Melvas, having sung themselves hoarse with their own praises, subsided one by one into drunken sleep, Taliesin, sitting near the great central fire, and throwing around a scrutinizing glance on all the objects in the hall, noticed a portly and somewhat elderly personage, of an aspect that would have been venerable, if it had been less rubicund and Bacchic, who continued plying his potations with undiminished energy, while the heroes of the festival dropped round him, like the leaves of autumn. This figure excited Taliesin's curiosity. This figure excited Taliesin's curiousity. The features struck him with a sense of resemblance to objects which had been somewhere familiar to him; but he perplexed himself in vain, with attempts at definite recollections. At length, when these two were almost the sole survivors of the evening, the stranger approached him with a golden goblet, which he had just replenished with the choicest wine of the vaults of Dinas Vawr, and pronounced the oracular monosyllable, "Drink!" to which he subjoined emphatically "GWIN O EUR: Wine from gold. That is my taste. Ale is well; mead is better; wine is best. Horn is well; silver is better; gold is best."

Taliesin, who had been very abstemious during the evening, took the golden goblet, and drank to please the inviter; in the hope that he would become communicative, and satisfy the curiosity his appearance had raised.

The stranger sat down near him, evidently in that amiable state of semi-intoxication which inflates the head, warms the heart, lifts up the veil of the inward man, and sets the tongue flying, or rather tripping, in the double sense of nimbleness and titubancy.

The stranger repeated, taking a copious draught, "My taste is wine from gold."

"I have heard those words," said Taliesin, "GWIN O EUR, repeated as having been the favorite saying of a person whose memory is fondly cherished by one as dear to me as a mother, though his name, with all others, is the by-word of all that is disreputable.

"I cannot believe," said the stranger, "that a man whose favorite saying was GWIN O EUR could possibily be a disreputable person, or deserve any other than that honourable remembrance, which, you say, only one person is honest enough to entertain for him."

"His name," said Taliesin, "is too unhappily notorious throughout Britain, by the terrible catastrophe of which his GWIN O EUR was the cause."

"And what might that be?" said the stranger.

"The inundation of Gwaelod," said Taliesin.

"You speak then," said the stranger, taking an enormous potation, "of Seithenyn, Prince Seithenyn, Seithenyn ap Seithin Saidi, Arglwyd Gorwarcheidwad yr Argae Breninawl."

"I seldom hear his name," said Taliesin, "with any of those sounding additions; he is usually called Seithenyn the Drunkard."

The stranger goggled about his eyes in an attempt to fix them steadily on Taliesin, screwed up the corners of his mouth, stuck out his nether lip, pursed up his chin, thrust forward his right foot, and elevated his golden goblet in his right hand; then, in a tone which he intended to be strongly becoming of his impressive aspect and imposing attitude, he muttered, "Look at me."

Taliesin looked at him accordingly, with as much gravity as he could preserve.

After a silence, which he designed to be very dignified and solemn, the stranger spoke again: "I am the man."

"What man?" said Taliesin.

"The man," replied his entertainer, "of whom you have spoken so disparagingly; Seithenyn ap Seithyn Saidi."

"Seithenyn," said Taliesin, "has slept twenty years under the waters of the western sea, as King Gwythno's Lamentations have made known to all Britain."

"They have not made it know to me," said Seithenyn, "for the best of all reasons, that one can only know the truth; for, if that which we think we know is not truth, it is something which we do not know. A man cannot know his own death; for, while he knows any thing, he is alive; at least, I never heard of a dead man who knew any thing, or pretended to know any thing: if he had so pretended, I should have told him to his face he was no dead man."

"Your mode of reasoning," said Taliesin, "unquestionably corresponds with what I have heard of Seithenyn's: but how is it possible Seithenyn can be living?"

"Every thing that is, is possible, says Catog the Wise; "answered Seithenyn, with a look of great sapience. "I will give you proof that I am not a dead man; for, they say, dead men tell no tales: now I will tell you a tale, and a very interesting one it is. When I saw the sea sapping the tower, I jumped into the water, and just in the nick of time. It was well for me that I have been so provident as to empty so many barrels, and that somebody, I don't know who, but I suppose it was my daughter, had been so provident as to put the bungs into them, to keep them sweet; for the beauty of it was that, when there was so much water in the case, it kept them empty; and when I jumped into the sea, the sea was just making a great hole in the cellar, and they were floating out by dozens. I don't know how I managed it, but I got one arm over one, and the other arm over another: I nipped them pretty tight; and, though my legs were under water, the good liquor I had in me kept me warm. I could not help thinking, as I had nothing else to think of just then that touched me so nearly, that if I had left them full, and myself empty, as a sober man would have done, we should all three, that is, I and the two barrels, have gone to the bottom together, that is to say, separately; for we should never have come together, except at the bottom, perhaps; when no one of us could have done the other any good; whereas they have done me much good, and I have requited it; for, first, I did them the service of emptying them; and then they did me the service of floating me with the tide, whether the ebb, or the flood, or both, is more than I can tell, down to the coast of Dyfed, where I was picked up by fishermen; and such was my sense of gratitude, that, though I had always before detested an empty barrel, except as a trophy, I swore I would not budge from the water unless my two barrels went with me; so we were all marched inland together, and were taken into the service of King Ednyfed, where I stayed till his castle was sacked, and his head cut off, and his beeves marched away with, by the followers of King Melvas, of whom I killed two or three; but they were too many for us: therefore, to make the best of a bad bargain, I followed leisurely in the train of the beeves, and presented myself to King Melvas, with this golden goblet, saying GWIN O EUR. He was struck with my deportment, and made me his chief butler; and now my two barrels are the two pillars of his cellar, where I regularly fill them from affection, and as regularly empty them from gratitude, taking care to put the bungs in them, to keep them sweet."

"But all this while," said Taliesin, "did you never look back to the Plain of Gwaelod, to your old king, and, above all, to your daughter?"

"Why yes," said Seithenyn, "I did in a way! But as to the Plain of Gwaelod, that was gone, buried under the sea, along with many good barrels, which I had been improvident enough to leave full: then, as to the old king, though I had a great regard for him, I thought he might be less likely to feast me in his hall, than to set up my head on a spike over his gate: then, as to my daughter—-"

Here he shook his head, and looked maudlin; and dashing two or three drops from his eye, he put a great many into his mouth.

"Your daughter," said Taliesin, "is the wife of King Elphin, and has a daughter, who is now as beautiful as her mother was."

"Very likely," said Seithenyn, "and I should be very glad to see them all; but I am afraid King Elphin, as you call him, (what he is king of, you shall tell me at leisure,) would do me a mischief. At any rate, he would stint me in liquor. No! If they will visit me, here I am. Fish, and water, will not agree with me. I am growing old, and need cordial nutriment. King Melvas will never want for beeves and wine; nor, indeed, for any thing else that is good. I can tell you what," he added, in a very low voice, cocking his eye, and putting his finger on his lips, "he has got in this very castle the finest woman in Britain."

"That I doubt," said Taliesin.

"She is the greatest, at any rate," said Seithenyn, "and ought to be the finest."

"How the greatest?" said Taliesin.

Seithenyn looked round, to observe if there were any listener near, and fixed a very suspicious gaze on a rotund figure of a fallen hero, who lay coiled up like a maggot in a filbert, and snoring with an energy that, to the muddy apprehensions of Seithenyn, seemed to be counterfeit. He determined, by a gentle experiment, to ascertain if his suspicions were well founded; and proceeded, with what he thought great caution, to apply the point of his foot to the most bulging portion of the fat sleeper's circumference. But he greatly mis-calculated his intended impetus, for he impinged his foot with a force that overbalanced himself, and hurled him headlong over his man, who instantly sprang on his legs, shouting "To arms!" Numbers started up at the cry; the hall rang with the din of arms, and with the vociferation of questions, which there were many to ask, and none to answer. Some stared about for the enemy; some rushed to the gates; others to the walls. Two or three, reeling in the tumult and the darkness, were jostled over the parapet, and went rolling down the precipitous slope of the castle hill, crashing through the bushes, and bellowing for some one to stop them, till their clamours were cut short by a plunge into the Towy, where the conjoint weight of their armour and their liquor carried them at once to the bottom. The rage which would have fallen on the enemy, if there had been one, was turned against the author of the false alarm; but, as none could point him out, the tumult subsided by degrees, through a descending scale of imprecations, into the last murmured malediction of him whom the intensity of his generous anger kept longest awake. By this time, the rotund hero had again coiled himself up into his ring; and Seithenyn was stretched in a right line, as a tangent to the circle, in a state of utter incapacity to elucidate the mystery of King Melvas's possession of the finest woman in Britain.

CHAPTER XII
The Splendour of Caer Lleon

The three principal cities of the isle of Britain: Caer Llion upon Wysg in Cymru; Caer Llundain in Lloegr; and Caer Evrawg in Deifr and Brynaich. * — *Triads of the Isle of Britain.*

THE SUNSET of a bright December day was glittering on the waves of the Usk, and on the innumerable roofs, which, being composed chiefly of the glazed tiles of the Romans, reflected the light almost as vividly as the river; when Taliesin descended one of the hills that border the beautiful valley in which then stood Caer Lleon, the metropolis of Britain, and in which now stands, on a small portion of the selfsame space, a little insignificant town, possessing nothing of its ancient glory but the unaltered name of Caer Lleon.

The rapid Usk flowed then, as now, under the walls: the high wooden bridge, with its slender piles, was then much the same as it is at this day: it seems to have been never regularly rebuilt, but to have been repaired, from time to time, on the original Roman model. The same green and fertile meadows, the same gently-sloping wood-covered hills, that now meet the eye of the tourist, the met the eye of Taliesin; except that the woods on one side of the valley, were then only the skirts of an extensive forest, which the nobility and beauty of Caer Lleon made frequently re-echo to the clamours of the chace.

The city, which had been so long the centre of the Roman supremacy, which was now the seat of the most illustrious sovereign that had yet held the sceptre of Britain, could not be approached by the youthful bard, whose genius was destined to eclipse that of all his countrymen, without feelings and reflections of deep interest. The sentimental tourist, (who, perching himself on an old wall, works himself up into a soliloquy of philosophical pathos, on the vicissitudes of empire and the mutability of all sublunary things, interrupted only by an occasional peep at his watch, to ensure his not overstaying the minute at which his fowl, comfortably roasting at the nearest inn, has been promised to be ready,) has, no doubt, many fine thoughts well worth recording in a dapper volume; but Taliesin had an interest in the objects before him too deep to have a thought to spare, even for his dinner. The monuments of Roman magnificence, and of Roman domination, still existing in comparative freshness; the arduous struggle, in which his countrymen were then engaged with the Saxons, and which, notwithstanding the actual triumphs of Arthur, Taliesin's prophetic spirit told him would end in their being dispossessed of all the land of Britain, except the wild region of Wales, (a result which political sagacity might have apprehended from their disunion, but which, as he told it to his countrymen in that memorable prophecy which every child of the Cymry knows, has established for him, among them, the fame of the prophet;) the importance to himself and his benefactors of the objects of his visit to the city, on the result of which depended the liberation of Elphin, and the success of his love for Melanghel; the degree in which these objects might be promoted by the construction he had put on Seithenyn's imperfect communication respecting the lady in Dinas Vawr; furnished, altogether, more materials for absorbing thought, than the most zealous peregrinator, even if he be at once poet, antiquary, and philosopher, is likely to have at once in his mind, on the top of the finest old wall on the face of the earth.

Taliesin passed, in deep musing, through the gates of Caer Lleon; but his attention was speedily drawn to the objects around him. From the wild solitudes in which he had passed his earlier years, the transition to the castles and cities he had already visited furnished much food to curiosity: but the ideas of them sunk into comparative nothingness before the magnificence of Caer Lleon.

He did not stop in the gateway to consider the knotty question, which had since puzzled so many antiquaries, whether the name of Caer Lleon signifies the City of Streams, the City of Legions, or the City of King Lleon? He saw a river filled with ships, flowing through fine meadows, bordered by hills and forests; walls of brick, as well as of stone; a castle, of impregnable strength; stately houses, of the most admirable architecture; palaces, with gilded roofs; Roman temples, and Christian churches; a theatre, and an amphitheatre. The public and private buildings of the departed Romans were in excellent preservation; though the buildings, and especially the temples, were no longer appropriated to their original purposes. The king's butler, Bedwyr, had taken possession of the Temple of Diana, as a cool place of deposit for wine: he had recently effected a stowage of vast quantities therein, and had made a most luminous arrangement of the several kinds; under the judicious and experience a super-intendence of Dyvrig, the Ex-Archbishop of Caer Lleon; who had just then nothing else to do, having recently resigned his see in favor of King Arthur's uncle, David, who is, to this day, illustrious as the St. David in whose honour the Welshmen annually adorn their hats with a leek. This David was a very respectable character in his way: he was a man of great sanctity and simplicity; and, in order to eschew the vanities of the world, which were continually present to him in Caer Lleon, he removed the metropolitan see, from Caer Lleon, to the rocky, barren, woodless, streamless, meadowless, tempest-beaten point of Mynyw, which was afterwards called St. David's. He was the mirror and pattern of a godly life; teaching by example, as by precept; admirable in words, and excellent in deeds; tall in stature, handsome in aspect, noble in deportment, affable in address, eloquent and learned, a model to his followers, the life of the poor, the protector of widows, and the father of orphans. This makes altogether a very respectable saint; and it cannot be said, that the honourable leek is unworthily consecrated. A long series of his Catholic successors maintained, in great magnificence, a cathedral, a college, and a palace; keeping them all in repair, and feeding the poor into the bargain, from the archiepiscopal, or, when the primacy of Caer Lleon had merged in that of Canterbury, from the episcopal, revenues; but these things were reformed altogether by one of the first Protestant bishops, who, having a lady that longed for the gay world, and wanting more than all the revenues for himself and his family, first raised the wind by selling off the lead from the roof of his palace, and then obtained permission to remove from it, on the plea that it was not watertight. The immediate successors of this bishop, whose name was Barlow, were in every way worthy of him; the palace and college have, consequently, fallen into incurable dilapidation, and the cathedral has fallen partially into ruins, and, most impartially, into neglect and defacement.

To return to Taliesin, in the streets of Caer Lleon. Plautus and Terence were not heard in the theatre, nor to be heard of in its neighbourhood; but it was thought an excellent place for an Eisteddfod, or Bardic Congress, and was made the principal place of assembly of the Bards of the island of Britain. This is what Ross of Warwick means, when he says there was a noble university of students in Caer Lleon.

The mild precepts of the new religion had banished the ferocious sports to which the Romans had dedicated the amphitheatre, and, as Taliesin passed, it was pouring forth an improved and humanized multitude, who had been enjoying the pure British pleasure of baiting a bear.

The hot baths and aqueducts, the stoves of "wonderful artifice," as Giraldus has it, which diffused hot air through narrow spiracles, and many other wonders of the place, did not all present themselves to a first observation. The streets were thronged with people, especially of the fighting order, of whom a greater number flocked about Arthur, than he always found it convenient to pay. Horsemen, with hawks and hounds, were returning from the neighbouring forest, accompanied by beautiful huntresses, in scarlet and gold.

Taliesin, having perlustrated the city, proceeded to the palace of Arthur. At the gates he was challenged by a formidable guard, but passed by his bardic privilege. It was now very near Christmas, and when Taliesin entered the great hall, it was blazing with artificial light, and glowing with the heat of the Roman stoves.

Arthur had returned victorious from the great battle of Badon hill, in which he had slain with his own hand four hundred and forty Saxons; and was feasting as merrily as an honest man can be supposed to do while his wife is away. Kings, princes, and soldiers of fortune, bards and prelates, ladies superbly apparelled, and many of them surpassingly beautiful; and a most gallant array of handsome young cupbearers, marshalled and well drilled by the king's butler, Bedwyr, who was himself a petty king, were the chief components of the illustrious assembly.

Amongst the ladies were the beautiful Tegau Eurvron; Dywir the Golden-haired; Enid, the daughter of Yniwl; Garwen, the daughter of Henyn; Gwyl, the daughter of Enddaud; and Indeg the daughter of Avarwy Hir, of Maelienydd. Of these, Tegau Eurvron, or Tegau of the Golden Bosom, was the wife of Caradoc, and one of the Three Chaste Wives of the island of Britain. She is the heroine, who, as the lady of Sir Cradock, is distinguished above all the ladies of Arthur's court, in the ballad of the Boy and the Mantle. [*]

Amongst the bards were Prince Llywarch, then in his youth, afterwards called Llywarch Hên, or Llywarch the Aged; Aneurin, the British Homer, who sang the fatal battle of Cattraëth, which laid the foundation of the Saxon ascendancy, in heroic numbers, which the gods have preserved to us, and who was called the Monarch of the Bards, before the days of the glory of Taliesin; and Merddin Gwyllt, or Merlin the Wild, who was so deep in the secrets of nature, that he obtained the fame of a magician, to which he had at least as good a title as either Friar Bacon or Cornelius Agrippa.

Amongst the petty kings, princes, and soldiers of fortune, were twenty-four marchawg, or cavaliers, who were the counsellors and champions of Arthur's court. This was the heroic band, illustrious, in the songs of chivalry, as the Knights of the Round Table. Their names and pedigrees would make a very instructive and entertaining chapter; and would include the interesting characters of Gwalchmai ap Gwyar the Courteous, the nephew of Arthur; Caradoc, "Colfn Cymry," the Pillar of Cambria, whose lady, as above noticed, was the mirror of chastity; and Trystan ap Tallwch, the lover of the beautiful Essyllt, the daughter, or, according to some, the wife, of his uncle March ap Meirchion; persons known to all the world, as Sir Gawain, Sir Cradock, and Sir Tristram.

On the right hand of King Arthur sate the beautiful Indeg, and on his left the lovely Garwen. Taliesin advanced, along the tesselated floor, towards the upper end of the hall, and, kneeling before King Arthur, said, "What boon will King Arthur grant to him who brings news of his queen?"

"Any boon," said Arthur, "that a king can give."

"Queen Gwenyvar," said Taliesin, "is the prisoner of King Melvas, in the castle of Dinas Vawr."

The mien and countenance of his informant satisfied the king that he knew what he was saying; therefore, without further parlance, he broke up the banquet, to make preparations for assailing Dinas Vawr.

But, before he began his march, King Melvas had shifted his quarters, and passed beyond the Severn to the isle of Avallon, where the marshes and winter-floods assured him some months of tranquillity and impunity.

King Arthur was highly exasperated, on receiving the intelligence of Melvas's movement; but he had no remedy, and was reduced to the alternative of making the best of his Christmas with the ladies, princes, and bards who crowded his court.

The period of the winter solstice had been always a great festival with the northern nations, the commencement of the lengthening of the days being, indeed, of all points in the circle of the year, that in which the inhabitants of cold countries have most cause to rejoice. This great festival was anciently called Yule; whether derived from the Gothic Iola, to make merry; or from the Celtic Hiaul, the sun; or from the Danish and Swedish Hiul, signifying wheel or revolution, December being Hiul-month, or the month of return; or from the Cimbric word Ol, which has the important signification of ALE, is too knotty a controversy to be settled here: but Yule had been long a great festival, with both Celts and Saxons; and, with the change of religion, became the great festival of Christmas, retaining most of its ancient characteristics while England was Merry England; a phrase which must be a mirifical puzzle to any one who looks for the first time on its present most lugubrious inhabitants.

The mistletoe of the oak was gathered by the Druids with great ceremonies, as a symbol of the season. The mistletoe continued to be so gathered, and to be suspended in halls and kitchens, if not in temples, implying an unlimited privilege of kissing; which circumstance, probably, led a learned antiquary to opine that it was the forbidden fruit.

The Druids, at this festival, made, in a capacious cauldron, a mystical brewage of carefully-selected ingredients, full of occult virtues, which they kept from the profane, and which was typical of the new year and of the transmigration of the soul. The profane, in humble imitation, brewed a bowl of spiced ale, or wine, throwing therein roasted crabs; the hissing of which, as they plunged, piping hot, into the liquor, was heard with much unction at midwinter, as typical of the conjunct benignant influences of fire and strong drink. The Saxons called this the Wassail-bowl, and the brewage of it is reported to have been one of the charms with which Rowena fascinated Vortigern.

King Arthur kept his Christmas so merrily, that the memory of it passed into a proverb: * "As merry as Christmas in Caer Lleon."

Caer Lleon was the merriest of places, and was commonly known by the name of Merry Caer Lleon; which the English ballad-makers, for the sake of the smoother sound, and confounding Cambria with Cumbria, most ignorantly or audaciously turned into Merry Carlisle; thereby emboldening a northern antiquary to set about proving that King Arthur was a Scotchman; according to the old principles of harry and foray, which gave Scotchmen a right to whatever they could find on the English border; though the English never admitted their title to any thing there, excepting a halter in Carlisle.

The chace, in the neighbouring forest; tilting in the amphitheatre; trials of skill of archery, in throwing the lance and riding at the quintain, and similar amusements of the morning, created good appetites for the evening feasts; in which Prince Cei, who is well known as Sir Kay, the seneschal, superintended the viands, as King Bedwyr did the liquor; having each a thousand men at command, for their provision, arrangement, and distribution; and music worthy of the banquet was provided and superintended by the king's chief harper, Geraint, of whom a contemporary poet observes, that when he died, the gates of heaven were thrown wide open, to welcome the ingress of so divine a musician.

CHAPTER XIII
The Ghostliness of Avallon

Poco piu poco meno, tutti al mondo vivono d'impostura: e
chi e di buon gusto, dissimula quando occorre, gode quando
puo, crede quel che vuole, ride de' pazzi. e figura un mondo
a suo gusto. —GOLDONI. *

"WHERE is the young bard," said Arthur, after some nights of
Christmas had passed by, "who brought me the news of my queen,
and to whom I promised a boon, which he has not yet claimed?"

None could satisfy the king's curiousity. Taliesin had disappeared
from Caer Lleon. He knew the power and influence of Maelgon
Gwyneth; and he was aware that King Arthur, however favorably he
might receive his petition, would not find leisure to compel the
liberation of Elphin, till he had enforced from Melvas the surrender
of his queen. It occurred to him that her restoration might be effected
by peaceable means; and he knew that, if he could be in any degree
instrumental to this result, it would greatly strengthen his claims on
the king. He engaged a small fishing-vessel, which had just landed a
cargo for the Christmas feasts of Caer Lleon, and set sail for the isle
of Avallon. At that period, the springtides of the sea rolled round a
cluster of islands, of which Avallon was one, over the extensive fens,
which wiser generations have embanked and reclaimed.

The abbey of Avallon, afterwards called Glastonbury, was, even
then, a comely and commodious pile, though not possessing any of
that magnificence which the accumulated wealth of ages
subsequently gave to it. A large and strongly fortified castle, almost
adjoining the abbey, gave the entire place the air of a strong hold of
the church militant. King Melvas was one of the pillars of the
orthodoxy of those days: he was called the Scrouge of the Pelagians;
and extended the shield of his temporal might over the spiritual
brotherhood of Avallon, who, in return, made it a point of
conscience not to stint him in absolutions.

The Misfortunes of Elphin

Some historians pretend that a comfortable nunnery was erected at a convenient distance from the abbey, that is to say, close to it; but this involves a nice question in monastic antiquity, which the curious may settle for themselves.

It was about midway between nones and vespers when Taliesin sounded, on the gate of the abbey, a notice of his wish for admission. A small trap-door in the gate was cautiously opened, and a face, as round and as red as the setting sun in November, shone forth in the aperture.

The topographers who have perplexed themselves about the origin of the name Ynys Avallon, "the island of apples," had not the advantage of this piece of meteoroscopy: if they could have looked on this archetype of a Norfolk beefin, with the knowledge that it was only a sample of a numerous fraternity, they would at once have perceived the fitness of the appellation. The brethren of Avallon were the apples of the church. It was the oldest monastic establishment in Britain; and consequently, as of reason, the most plump, succulent, and rosy. It had, even in the sixth century, put forth the fruits of good living, in a manner that would have done honour to a more enlightened age. It went on steadily improving in this line till the days of its last abbot, Richard Whiting, who built the stupendous kitchen, which has withstood the ravages of time and the Reformation; and who, as appears by authentic documents, and, amongst others, by a letter signed with the honoured name of Russell, was found guilty, by a right worshipful jury, of being suspected of great riches, and of an inclination to keep them; and was accordingly sentenced to be hanged forthwith, along with his treasurer and subtreasurer, who were charged with aiding and abetting him in the safe custody of his cash and plate; at the same time that the Abbot of Peterborough was specially reprieved from the gallows, on the ground that he was the said Russell's particular friend. This was a compendium of justice and mercy according to the new light of King Henry the Eighth. The abbot's kitchen is the most interesting and perfect portion of the existing ruins. These ruins were overgrown with the finest ivy in England, till it was, not long since, pulled down by some Vandal, whom the Society of Antiquaries had sent down to make drawings of the walls, which he executed literally, by stripping them bare, that he might draw the walls, and nothing else. Its shade no longer waves over the musing moralist, who, with folded arms, and his back against a wall, dreams of the days that are gone; or the sentimental cockney, who, seating himself with much gravity on a fallen column, produces a flute from his pocket, and strikes up "I'd be a butterfly." [*]

From the phænomenon of a blushing fruit that was put forth in the abbey gate of Avallon issued a deep, fat, gurgling voice, which demanded of Taliesin his name and business.

"I seek the abbot of Avallon," said Taliesin.

"He is confessing a penitent," said the ghostly brother, who was officiating in turn as porter.

"I can await his leisure," said Taliesin, "but I must see him."

"Are you alone?" said the brother.

"I am," said Taliesin.

The gate unclosed slowly, just wide enough to give him admittance. It was then again barred and barricadoed.

The ghostly brother, of whom Taliesin had now a full view, had a figure corresponding with his face, and wanted nothing but a pair of horns and a beard in ringlets, to look like an avatar of Bacchus. He maintained, however, great gravity of face, and decorum of gesture, as he said to Taliesin, "Hospitality is the rule of our house; but we are obliged to be cautious in these times, though we live under powerful protection. Those bloody Nimrods, the Saxons, are athirst for the blood of the righteous. Monsters that are born with tails."

Taliesin had not before heard of this feature of Saxon conformation, and expressed his astonishment accordingly.

"How?" said the monk. "Did not a rabble of them fasten goats" tails to the robe of the blessed preacher in Riw, and did he not, therefore, pray that their posterity might be born with tails? And it is so. But let that pass. Have they not sacked monasteries, plundered churches, and put holy brethren to the sword? The blood of the saints calls for vengeance."

"And will have it," said Taliesin, "from the hand of Arthur."

The name of Arthur evidently discomposed the monk, who, desiring Taliesin to follow him, led the way across the hall of the abbey, and along a short wide passage, at the end of which was a portly door.

The monk disappeared through this door, and, presently returning, said, "The abbot requires your name and quality."

"Taliesin, the bard of Elphin ap Gwythno Garanhir," was the reply.

The monk disappeared again, and, returning, after a longer pause than before, said, "You may enter."

The abbot was a plump and comely man, of middle age, having three roses in his complexion; one in full blossom on each cheek, and one in bud on the tip of his nose.

He was sitting at a small table, on which stood an enormous vase, and a golden goblet; and opposite to him sat the penitent of whom the round-faced brother had spoken, and in whom Taliesin recognised his acquaintance of Dinas Vawr, who called himself Seithenyn ap Seithyn.

The abbot and Seithenyn sat with their arms folded on the table, leaning forward towards each other, as if in momentous discussion.

The abbot said to Taliesin, "Sit;" and to his conductor, "Retire, and be silent."

"Will it not be better," said the monk, "that I cross my lips with the sign of secrecy?"

"It is permitted," said the abbot.

Seithenyn held forth the goblet to the monk, who swallowed the contents with much devotion. He then withdrew, and closed the door.

"I bid you most heartily welcome," said Seithenyn to Taliesin. "Drink off this, and I will tell you more. You are admitted to this special sitting at my special instance. I told the abbot I knew you well. Now I will tell you what I know. You have told King Arthur that King Melvas has possession of Queen Gwenyvar, and, in consequence, King Arthur is coming here, to sack and raze the castle and abbey, and cut every throat in the isle of Avallon. I have just brought the abbot this pleasant intelligence, and, as I knew it would take him down a cup or two, I have also brought what I call my little jug, to have the benefit of his judgment on a piece of rare wine which I have broached this morning: there is no better in Caer Lleon. And now we are holding council on the emergency. But I must say you abuse your bardic privilege, to enjoy people's hospitality, worm out of their secrets, and carry the news to the enemy. It was partly to give you this candid opinion, that I have prevailed on the abbot to admit you to this special sitting. Therefore drink. GWIN O EUR: Wine from gold."

"King Arthur is not a Saxon, at any rate," sighed the abbot, winding up his fainting spirits with a draught. "Think not, young stranger, that I am transgressing the laws of temperance: my blood runs so cold when I think of the blood-thirsty Saxons, that I take a little wine medicinally, in the hope of warming it; but it is a slow and tedious remedy."

"Take a little more," said Seithenyn. "That is the true quantity. Wine is my medicine; and my quantity is a little more. A little more."

"King Arthur," said Taliesin, "is not a Saxon; but he does not brook injuries lightly. It were better for your abbey that he came not here in arms. The aiders and abettors of Melvas, even though they be spiritual, may not carry off the matter without some share of his punishment, which is infallible."

"That is just what I have been thinking," said Seithenyn.

"God knows," said the abbot, "we are not abettors of Melvas, though we need his temporal power to protect us from the Saxons."

"How can it be otherwise," said Taliesin, "than that these Saxon despoilers should be insolent and triumphant, while the princes of Britain are distracted with domestic broils: and for what?"

"Ay," said Seithenyn, "that is the point. For what? For a woman, or some such rubbish."

"Rubbish, most verily," said the abbot. "Women are the flesh which we renounce with the devil."

"Holy father," said Taliesin, "have you not spiritual influence with Melvas, to persuade him to surrender the queen without bloodshed, and, renewing his allegiance to Arthur, assist him in his most sacred war against the Saxon invaders?"

"A righteous work," said the abbot; "but Melvas is headstrong and difficult."

"Screw yourself up with another goblet," said Seithenyn; "you will find the difficulty smooth itself off wonderfully. Wine from gold has a sort of double light, that illuminates a dark path miraculously."

The abbot sighed deeply, but adopted Seithenyn's method of throwing light on the subject.

The Misfortunes of Elphin

"The anger of King Arthur," said Taliesin, "is certain, and its consequences infallible. The anger of King Melvas is doubtful, and its consequences to you cannot be formidable."

"That is nearly true," said the abbot, beginning to look resolute, as the rosebud at his nose-tip deepened into damask.

"A little more," said Seithenyn, "and it will become quite true."

By degrees the proposition ripened into absolute truth. The abbot suddenly inflated his cheeks, started on his legs, and stalked bolt upright out of the apartment, and forthwith out of the abbey, followed by Seithenyn, tossing his goblet in the air, and catching it in his hand, as he went.

The round-faced brother made his appearance almost immediately. "The abbot," he said, "commends you to the hospitality of the brotherhood. They will presently assemble to supper. In the meanwhile, as I am thirsty, and content with whatever falls in my way, I will take a simple and single draught of what happens to be here."

His draught was a model of simplicity and singleness; for, having uplifted the ponderous vase, he held it to his lips, till he had drained it of the very copious remnant which the abrupt departure of the abbot had caused Seithenyn to leave in it.

Taliesin proceeded to enjoy the hospitality of the brethren, who set before him a very comfortable hot supper, at which he quickly perceived, that, however dexterous King Elphin might be at catching fish, the monks of Avallon were very far his masters in the three great arts of cooking it, serving it up, and washing it down; but he had not time to profit by their skill and experience in these matters, for he received a pressing invitation to the castle of Melvas, which he obeyed immediately.

CHAPTER XIV
The Right of Might

The three triumphs of the bards of the isle of Britain: the triumph of learning over ignorance; the triumph of reason over terror; and the triumph of peace over violence. — *Triads of Bardism.*

"FRIEND Seithenyn," said the abbot, when having passed the castle gates, and solicited an audience, he was proceeding to the presence of Melvas, "this task, to which I have accinged myself, is arduous, and in some degree awful; being, in truth, no less than to persuade a king to surrender a possession, which he has inclination to keep for ever, at any rate, for an indefinite time."

Not so very indefinite," said Seithenyn; "for with the first song of the cuckoo (whom I mention on this occasion as a party concerned,) King Arthur will batter his castle about his ears, and, in all likelihood, the abbey about yours."

The abbot sighed heavily.

"If your heart fail you," said Seithenyn, "another cup of wine will set all to rights."

"Nay, nay, friend Seithenyn," said the abbot, "that which I have already taken has just brought me to the point at which the heart is inspirited, and the wit sharpened, without any infraction of the wisdom and gravity which become my character, and best suit my present business."

Seithenyn, however, took an opportunity of making signs to some cupbearers, and, when they entered the apartment of Melvas, they were followed by vessels of wine and goblets of gold.

King Melvas was a man of middle age, with a somewhat round, large, regular-featured face, and an habitual smile of extreme self-satisfaction, which he could occasionally convert into a look of terrific ferocity, the more fearful for being rare. His manners were, for the most part, pleasant. He did much mischief, not for mischief's sake, nor yet for the sake of excitement, but for the sake of something tangible. He had a total and most complacent indifference to every thing but his own will and pleasure. He took what he wanted wherever he could find it, by the most direct process, and without any false pretence. He would have disdained the trick which the chroniclers ascribe to Hengist, of begging as much land as a bull's hide would surround, and then shaving it into threads, which surrounded a goodly space. If he wanted a piece of land, he encamped upon it, saying, "This is mine." If the former possessor could eject him, so; it was not his: if not, so; it remained his. Cattle, wine, furniture, another man's wife, whatever he took a fancy to, he pounced upon and appropriated. He was intolerant of resistance; and, as the shortest way of getting rid of it, and not from any blood-thirstiness of disposition, or, as the phrenologists have it, development of the organ of destructiveness, he always cut through the resisting body, longitudinally, horizontally, or diagonally, as he found most convenient. He was the arch-marauder of West Britain. The abbey of Avallon shared largely in the spoil, and they made up together a most harmonious church and state. He had some respect for King Arthur; wished him success against the Saxons; knew the superiority of his power to his own; but he had heard that Queen Gwenyvar was the most beautiful woman in Britain; was, therefore, satisfied of his own title to her, and, as she was hunting in the forest, while King Arthur was absent from Caer Lleon, he seized her, and carried her off.

"Be seated, holy father," said Melvas; "and you, also, Seithenyn, unless the abbot wishes you away."

But the abbot's heart misgave him, and he assented readily to Seithenyn's stay.

MELVAS:

Now, holy father, to your important matter of private conference.

SEITHENYN:

He is tongue-tied, and a cup too low.

THE ABBOT:

Set the goblet before me, and I will sip in moderation.

MELVAS:

Sip, or not sip, tell me your business.

THE ABBOT:

My business, of a truth, touches the lady your prisoner, King Arthur's queen.

MELVAS:

She is my queen, while I have her, and no prisoner. Drink, man, and be not afraid. Speak your mind: I will listen, and weigh your words.

THE ABBOT:

This queen—-

SEITHENYN:

Obey the king: first drink, then speak.

THE ABBOT:

I drink to please the king.

MELVAS:

Proceed.

THE ABBOT:

This queen, Gwenyvar, is as beautiful as Helen, who caused the fatal war that expelled our fore-fathers from Troy: and I fear she will be a second Helen, and expel their posterity from Britain.* The infidel Saxons, to whom the cowardly and perfidious Vortigern gave footing in Britain, have prospered even more by the disunion of her princes than either by his villany, or their own valour. And now there is no human hope against them but in the arms of Arthur. And how shall his arms prosper against the common enemy, if he be forced to turn them on the children of his own land for the recovery of his own wife?

MELVAS:

What do you mean by his own? That which he has, is his own: but that which I have, is mine. I have the wife in question, and some of the land. Therefore they are mine.

THE ABBOT:

Not so. The land is yours under fealty to him.

MELVAS:

As much fealty as I please, or he can force me, to give him.

THE ABBOT:

His wife, at least, is most lawfully his.

MELVAS:

The winner makes the law, and his law is always against the loser. I am so far the winner; and, by my own law, she is lawfully mine.

THE ABBOT:

There is a law above all human law, by which she is his.

MELVAS:

From that it is for you to absolve me; and I dispense my bounty according to your indulgence.

THE ABBOT:

There are limits we must not pass.

MELVAS:

You set up your landmark, and I set up mine. They are both moveable.

THE ABBOT:

The Church has not been niggardly in its indulgences to King Melvas.

MELVAS:

Nor King Melvas in his gifts to the Church.

THE ABBOT:

But, setting aside this consideration, I would treat it as a question of policy.

SEITHENYN:

Now you talk sense. Right without might is the lees of an old barrel, without a drop of the original liquor.

THE ABBOT:

I would appeal to you, King Melvas, by your love to your common country, by your love of the name of Britain, by your hatred of the infidel Saxons, by your respect of the character of Arthur; will you let your passion for a woman, even though she be a second Helen, frustrate, or even impede, the great cause, of driving these spoilers from a land in which they have no right even to breathe?

MELVAS:

They have a right to do all they do, and to have all they have. If we can drive them out, they will then have no right here. Have not you and I a right to this good wine, which seems to trip very merrily over your ghostly palate? I got it by seizing a good ship, and throwing the crew overboard, just to remove them out of the way, because they were troublesome. They disputed my right, but I taught them better. I taught them a great moral lesson, though they had not much time to profit by it. If they had had the might to throw me overboard, I should not have troubled myself about their right, any more, or, at any rate, any longer, than they did about mine.

SEITHENYN:

The wine was lawful spoil of war.

THE ABBOT:

But if King Arthur brings his might to bear upon yours, I fear neither you nor I shall have a right to this wine, nor to any thing else that is here.

SEITHENYN:

Then make the most of it while you have it.

THE ABBOT:

Now, while you have some months of security before you, you may gain great glory by surrendering the lady; and, if you be so disposed, you may no doubt claim, from the gratitude of King Arthur, the fairest princess of his court to wife, and an ample dower withal.

MELVAS:

That offers something tangible.

SEITHENYN:

Another ray from the golden goblet will set it in a most luminous view.

THE ABBOT:

Though I should advise the not making it a condition, but asking it, as a matter of friendship, after the first victory that you have helped him to gain over the Saxons.

MELVAS:

The worst of those Saxons is, that they offer nothing tangible, except hard knocks. They bring nothing with them. They come to take; and lately they have not taken much. But I will muse on your advice; and, as it seems, I may get more by following than rejecting it, I shall very probably take it, provided that you now attend me to the banquet in the hall.

SEITHENYN:

Now you talk of the hall and the banquet, I will just intimate that the finest of all youths, and the best of all bards, is a guest in the neighbouring abbey.

MELVAS:

If so, I have a clear right to him, as a guest for myself.

The abbot was not disposed to gainsay King Melvas's right. Taliesin was invited accordingly, and seated at the left hand of the king, the abbot being on the right. Taliesin summoned all the energies of his genius to turn the passions of Melvas into the channels of Anti-Saxonism, and succeeded so perfectly, that the king and his whole retinue of magnanimous heroes were inflamed with intense ardour to join the standard of Arthur; and Melvas vowed most solemnly to Taliesin, that another sun should not set, before Queen Gwenyvar should be under the most honourable guidance on her return to Caer Lleon.

CHAPTER XV
The Circle of the Bards

The three dignities of poetry: the union of the true and the wonderful; the union of the beautiful and the wise; and the union of art and nature. — *Triads of Poetry.*

AMONGST the Christmas amusements of Caer Lleon, a grand Bardic Congress was held in the Roman theatre, when the principal bards of Britain contended for the pre-eminence in the art of poetry, and in its appropriate moral and mystical knowledge. The meeting was held by daylight. King Arthur presided, being himself an irregular bard, and admitted, on this public occasion, to all the efficient honours of a Bard of Presidency.

To preside in the Bardic Congress was long a peculiar privilege of the kings of Britain. It was exercised in the seventh century by King Cadwallader. King Arthur was assisted by twelve umpires, chosen by the bards, and confirmed by the king.

The Court, of course, occupied the stations of honour, and every other part of the theatre was crowded with a candid and liberal audience.

The bards sate in a circle on that part of the theatre corresponding with the portion which we call the stage.

Silence was proclaimed by the herald; and, after a grand symphony, which was led off in fine style by the king's harper, Geraint, Prince Cei came forward, and made a brief oration, to the effect that any of the profane, who should be irregular and tumultuous, would be forcibly removed from the theatre, to be dealt with at the discretion of the officer of the guard. Silence was then a second time proclaimed by the herald.

Each bard, as he stood forward, was subjected to a number of interrogatories, metrical and mystical, which need not be here

reported. Many bards sang many songs. Amongst them, Prince
Llywarch sang

GORWYNION Y GAUAV.

THE BRILLIANCIES OF WINTER.

Last of flowers, in tufts around
Shines the gorse's golden bloom:
Milkwhite lichens clothe the ground
"Mid the flowerless heath and broom:
Bright are holly-berries, seen
Red, through leaves of glossy green.

Brightly, as on rocks they leap,
Shine the sea-waves, white with spray;
Brightly, in the dingles deep,
Gleams the river's foaming way;
Brightly through the distance show
Mountain-summits clothed in snow.

Brightly, where the torrents bound,
Shines the frozen colonnade,
Which the black rocks, dripping round,
And the flying spray have made:
Bright the icedrops on the ash
Leaning o'er the cataract's dash.

Bright the hearth, where feast and song
Crown the warrior's hour of peace,
While the snow-storm drives along,
Bidding the war's worse tempest cease;
Bright the hearthflame, flashing clear
On the up-hung shield and spear.

Bright the torchlight of the hall
When the wintry night-winds blow;
Brightness when its splendours fall

On the mead-cup's sparking flow:
While the maiden's smile of light
Makes the brightness trebly bright.

Close the portals; pile the hearth;
Strike the harp; the feast pursue;
Brim the horns: fire, music, mirth,
Mead and love, are winter's due.
Spring to purple conflict calls
Swords that shine on winter's walls.

Llywarch's song was applauded, as presenting a series of images
with which all present were familiar, and which were all of them
agreeable.

Merlin sang some verses of the poem which is called

AVALLENAU MYRDDIN.

MERLIN'S APPLE-TREES.

Fair the gift to Merlin given,
Apple-trees seven score and seven;
Equal all in age and size;
On a green hill-slope, that lies
Basking in the southern sun,
Where bright waters murmuring run.

Just beneath the pure stream flows;
High above the forest grows;
Not again on earth is found
Such a slope of orchard ground:
Song of birds, and hum of bees,
Ever haunt the apple-trees.

Lovely green their leaves in spring;
Lovely bright their blossoming:
Sweet the shelter and the shade

The Misfortunes of Elphin

By their summer foliage made:
Sweet the fruit their ripe boughs hold,
Fruit delicious, tinged with gold.

Gloyad, nymph with tresses bright,
Teeth of pearl, and eyes of light,
Guards these gifts of Ceidio's son,
Gwendol, the lamented one,
Him, whose keen-edged, sword no more
Flashes 'mid the battle's roar.

War has raged on vale and hill:
That fair grove was peaceful still.
There have chiefs and princes sought
Solitude and tranquil thought:
There have kings, from courts and throngs,
Turned to Merlin's wild-wood songs.

Now from echoing woods I hear
Hostile axes sounding near:
On the sunny slope reclined,
Feverish grief disturbs my mind,
Lest the wasting edge consume
My fair spot of fruit and bloom.

Lovely trees, that long alone
In the sylvan vale have grown,
Bare, your sacred plot around,
Grows the once wood-waving ground:
Fervent valour guards ye still;
Yet my soul presages ill.

Well I know, when years have flown,
Briars shall grow where ye have grown:
Them in turn shall power uproot;
Then again shall flowers and fruit
Flourish in the sunny breeze,
On my new-born apple-trees.

This song was heard with much pleasure, especially by those of the audience who could see, in the imagery of the apple-trees, a mystical type of the doctrines and fortunes of Druidism, to which Merlin was suspected of being secretly attached, even under the very nose of St. David.

Aneurin sang a portion of his poem on the battle of Cattraeth; in which he shadowed out the glory of Vortimer, the weakness of Vortigern, the fascinations of Rowena, the treachery of Hengist, and the vengeance of Emrys.

THE MASSACRE OF THE BRITONS

Sad was the day for Britain's land,
A day of ruin to the free,
When Gorthyn stretched a friendly hand
To the dark dwellers of the sea.

But not in pride the Saxon trod,
Nor force nor fraud oppressed the brave,
Ere the grey stone and flowery sod
Closed o'er the blessed hero's grave. *

The twice-raised monarch drank the charm,
The love-draught of the ocean-maid:
Vain then the Briton's heart and arm,
Keen spear, strong shield, and burnished blade.

"Come to the feast of wine and mead,"
Spake the dark dweller of the sea:
"There shall the hours of mirth proceed;
There neither sword nor shield shall be."

Hard by the sacred temple's site,
Soon as the shades of evening fall,
Resounds the song and glows with light
The ocean-dweller's rude-built hall.

The sacred ground, where chiefs of yore
The everlasting fire adored,
The solemn pledge of safety bore,
And breathed not of the treacherous sword.

The amber wreath his temples bound;
His vest concealed the murderous blade;
As man to man, the board around,
The guileful chief his host arrayed.

None but the noblest of the land,
The flower of Britain's chiefs, were there:
Unarmed, amid the Saxon band,
They sate, the fatal feast to share.

Three hundred chiefs, three score and three,
Went, where the festal torches burned
Before the dweller of the sea:
They went; and three alone returned.

"Till dawn the pale sweet mead they quaffed:
The ocean-chief unclosed his vest;
His hand was on his dagger's haft,
And daggers glared at every breast.

But him, at Eidiol's breast who aimed,
The mighty Briton's arm laid low:
His eyes with righteous anger flamed;
He wrenched the dagger from the foe;

And through the throng he cleft his way,
And raised without his battle cry;
And hundreds hurried to the fray,
From towns, and vales, and mountains high.

But Britain's best blood dyed the floor
Within the treacherous Saxon's hall;
Of all, the golden chain who wore,

The Misfortunes of Elphin

Two only answered Eidiol's call.

Then clashed the sword; then pierced the lance;
Then by the axe the shield was riven;
Then did the steel on Cattraeth prance,
And deep in blood his hoofs were driven.

Even as the flame consumes the wood,
So Eidiol rushed along the field:
As sinks the snow-bank in the flood,
So did the ocean-rovers yield.

The spoilers from the fane he drove;
He hurried to the rock-built tower,
Where the base king, in mirth and love,
Sate with his Saxon paramour.

The storm of arms was on the gate,
The blaze of torches in the hall,
So swift, that ere they feared their fate,
The flames had scaled their chamber wall.

They died: for them no Briton grieves;
No planted flower above them waves;
No hand removes the withered leaves
That strew their solitary graves.

And time the avenging day brought round
That saw the sea-chief vainly sue:
To make his false host bite the ground
Was all the hope our warrior knew.

And evermore the strife he led,
Disdaining peace, with princely might,
Till, on a spear, the spoiler's head
Was reared on Caer-y-Cynan's height.

The song of Aneurin touched deeply on the sympathies of the audience, and was followed by a grand martial symphony, in the midst of which Taliesin appeared in the Circle of Bards. King Arthur welcomed him with great joy, and sweet smiles were showered upon him from all the beauties of the court.

Taliesin answered the metrical and mystical questions to the astonishment of the most proficient; and, advancing, in his turn, to the front of the circle, he sang a portion of a poem which is now called HANES TALIESIN, the History of Taliesin; but which shall be here entitled

THE CAULDRON OF CERIDWEN

The sage Ceridwen was the wife
Of Tegid Voël, of Pemble Mere:
Two children blest their wedded life,
Morvran and Creirwy, fair and dear:
Morvran, a son of peerless worth,
And Creirwy, loveliest nymph of earth:
But one more son Ceridwen bare,
As foul as they before were fair.

She strove to make Avagddu wise;
She knew he never could be fair:
And, studying magic mysteries,
She gathered plants of virtue rare:
She placed the gifted plants to steep
Within the magic cauldron deep,
Where they a year and day must boil,
"Till three drops crown the matron's toil.

Nine damsels raised the mystic flame;
Gwion the Little near it stood:
The while for simples roved the dame
Though tangled dell and pathless wood.
And, when the year and day had past,
The dame within the cauldron cast

The consummating chaplet wild,
While Gwion held the hideous child.

But from the cauldron rose a smoke
That filled with darkness all the air:
When through its folds the torchlight broke,
Nor Gwion, nor the boy, was there.
The fire was dead, the cauldron cold,
And in it lay, in sleep uprolled.
Fair as the morning-star, a child,
That woke, and stretched its arms, and smiled.

What chanced her labours to destroy,
She never knew; and sought in vain
If 'twere her own misshapen boy,
Or little Gwion, born again:
And vexed with doubt, the babe she rolled
In cloth of purple and of gold,
And in a coracle consigned
Its fortunes to the sea and wind.

The summer night was still and bright,
The summer moon was large and clear,
The frail bark, on the springtide's height,
Was floated into Elphin's weir:
The baby in his arms he raised:
His lovely spouse stood by, and gazed,
And, blessing it with gentle vow,
Cried "TALIESIN!" "Radiant brow!"

And I am he: and well I know
Ceridwen's power protects me still;
And hence o'er hill and vale I go,
And sing, unharmed, whate"er I will.
She has for me Time's veil withdrawn:
The images of things long gone,
The shadows of the coming days,
Are present to my visioned gaze.

And I have heard the words of power,
By Ceirion's solitary lake,
That bid, at midnight's thrilling hour,
Eryri's hundred echoes wake.
I to Diganwy's towers have sped,
And now Caer Lleon's halls I tread,
Demanding justice, now, as then,
From Maelgon, most unjust of men.

The audience shouted with delight at the song of Taliesin, and King Arthur, as President of the Bardic Congress, conferred on him, at once, the highest honours of the sitting.

Where Taliesin picked up the story which he told of himself, why he told it, and what he meant by it, are questions not easily answered. Certain it is, that he told this story to his contemporaries, and that none of them contradicted it. It may, therefore, be presumed that they believed it; as any one who pleases is most heartily welcome to do now.

Besides the single songs, there were songs in dialogue, approaching very nearly to the character of dramatic poetry; and pennillion, or unconnected stanzas, sung in series by different singers, the stanzas being complete in themselves, simple as Greek epigrams, and presenting in succession moral precepts, pictures of natural scenery, images of war or of festival, the lamentations of absence or captivity, and the complaints or triumphs of love. This pennillion-singing long survived among the Welsh peasantry almost every other vestige of bardic customs, and may still be heard among them on the few occasions on which rack-renting, tax-collecting, common-enclosing, methodist-preaching, and similar developments of the light of the age, have left them either the means or inclination of making merry.

CHAPTER XVI
The Judgments of Arthur

Three things to which success cannot fail where they shall
justly be: discretion, exertion, and hope. — *Triads of Wisdom.*

KING Arthur had not long returned to his hall, when Queen
Gwenyvar arrived, escorted by the Abbot of Avallon and Seithenyn
ap Seithyn Saidi, who had brought his golden goblet, to gain a new
harvest of glory from the cellars of Caer Lleon.

Seithenyn assured King Arthur, in the name of King Melvas, and on
the word of a king, backed by that of his butler, which, truth being in
wine, is good warranty even for a king, that the queen returned as
pure as on the day King Melvas had carried her off.

"None here will doubt that;" said Gwenvach, the wife of Modred.
Gwenyvar was not pleased with the compliment, and, almost before
she had saluted King Arthur, she turned suddenly round, and
slapped Gwenvach on the face, with a force that brought more
crimson in one cheek than blushing had ever done into both. This
slap is recorded in the Bardic Triads as one of the Three Fatal Slaps
of the Island of Britain. A terrible effect is ascribed to this small
cause; for it is said to have been the basis of that enmity between
Arthur and Modred, which terminated in the battle of Camlan,
wherein all the flower of Britain perished on both sides: a
catastrophe more calamitous than any that ever before or since
happened in Christendom, not even excepting that of the battle of
Roncesvalles; for, in the battle of Camlan, the Britons exhausted their
own strength, and could no longer resist the progress of the Saxon
supremacy. This, however, was a later result, and comes not within
the scope of the present veridicous narrative.

Gwenvach having flounced out of the hall, and the tumult
occasioned by this little incident having subsided, Queen Gwenyvar
took her ancient seat by the side of King Arthur, who proceeded to
inquire into the circumstances of her restoration. The Abbot of

Avallon began an oration, in praise of his own eloquence, and its miraculous effects on King Melvas; but he was interrupted by Seithenyn, who said, "The abbot's eloquence was good and well timed; but the chief merit belongs to this young bard, who prompted him with good counsel, and to me, who inspirited him with good liquor. If he had not opened his mouth pretty widely when I handed him this golden goblet, exclaiming GWIN O EUR, he would never have had the heart to open it to any other good purpose. But the most deserving person is this very promising youth, in whom I can see no fault, but that he has not the same keen perception as my friend the abbot has of the excellent relish of wine from gold. To be sure, he plied me very hard with strong drink in the hall of Dinas Vawr, and thereby wormed out of me the secret of Queen Gwenyvar's captivity; and, afterwards, he pursued us to Avallon, where he persuaded me and the abbot, and the abbot persuaded King Melvas, that it would be better for all parties to restore the queen peaceably: and then he clenched the matter with the very best song I ever heard in my life. And, as my young friend has a boon to ask, I freely give him all my share of the merit, and the abbot's into the bargain."

"Allow me, friend GWIN O EUR," said the abbot, "to dispose of my own share of merit in my own way. But, such as it is, I freely give it to this youth, in whom, as you say, I can see no fault, but that his head is brimfull of Pagan knowledge."

Arthur paid great honour to Taliesin, and placed him on his left hand at the banquet. He then said to him, "I judge, from your song of this morning, that the boom you require from me concerns Maelgon Gwyneth. What is his transgression, and what is the justice you require?"

Taliesin narrated the adventures of Elphin in such a manner as gave Arthur an insight into his affection for Melanghel; and he supplicated King Arthur to command and enforce the liberation of Elphin from the Stone Tower of Diganwy.

The Misfortunes of Elphin

Before King Arthur could signify his assent, Maelgon Gwyneth stalked into the hall, followed by a splendid retinue. He had been alarmed by the absence of Rhûn, had sought him in vain on the banks of Mawddach, had endeavoured to get at the secret by pouncing upon Angharad and Melanghel, and had been baffled in his project by the vigilance of Teithrin ap Tathral. He had, therefore, as a last resort, followed Taliesin to Caer Lleon, conceiving that he might have had some share in the mysterious disappearance of Rhûn.

Arthur informed him that he was in possession of all the circumstances, and that Rhûn, who was in safe custody, would be liberated on the restoration of Elphin.

Maelgon boiled with rage and shame, but had no alternative but submission to the will of Arthur.

King Arthur commanded that all the parties should be brought before him. Caradoc was charged with the execution of this order, and, having received the necessary communications and powers from Maelgon and Taliesin, he went first to Diganwy, where he liberated Elphin, and then proceeded to give effect to Teithrin's declaration, that "no hand but Elphin's should raise the stone of Rhûn's captivity." Rhûn, while his pleasant adventure had all the gloss of novelty upon it, and his old renown as a gay deceiver was consequently in such dim eclipse, was very unwilling to present himself before the ladies of Caer Lleon; but Caradoc was peremptory, and carried off the crest-fallen prince, together with his bard of all work, who was always willing to go to any court, with any character, or none.

Accordingly, after a moderate lapse of time, Caradoc reappeared in the hall of Arthur, with the liberated captives, accompanied by Angharad and Melanghel, and Teithrin ap Tathral.

King Arthur welcomed the new comers with a magnificent festival, at which all the beauties of his court were present, and, addressing himself to Elphin, said, "We are all debtors to this young bard: my queen and myself for her restoration to me; you for your liberation from the Stone Tower of Dignawy. Now, if there be, amongst all

101

these ladies, one whom he would choose for his bride, and in whose eyes he may find favor, I will give the bride a dowry worthy of the noblest princess in Britain."

Taliesin, thus encouraged, took the hand of Melanghel, who did not attempt to withdraw it, but turned to her father a blushing face, in which he read her satisfaction and her wishes. Elphin immediately said, "I have nothing to give him but my daughter; but her I most cordially give him."

Taliesin said, "I owe to Elphin more than I can ever repay: life, honour, and happiness."

Arthur said, "You have not paid him ill; but you owe nothing to Maelgon and Rhûn, who are your debtors for a lesson of justice, which I hope they will profit by during the rest of their lives. Therefore Maelgon shall defray the charge of your wedding, which shall be the most splendid that has been seen in Caer Lleon."

Maelgon looked exceedingly grim, and wished himself well back in Diganwy.

There was a very pathetic meeting of recognition between Seithenyn and his daughter; at the end of which he requested her husband's interest to obtain for him the vacant post of second butler to King Athur. He obtained this honourable office; and he was so zealous in the fulfiment of its duties, that, unless on actual service with a detachment of liquor, he was never a minute absent from the Temple of Diana.

At a subsequent Bardic Congress, Taliesin was unanimously elected Pen Beirdd, or Chief of the Bards of Britain. The kingdom of Caredigion flourished under the protection of Arthur, and, in the ripeness of time, passed into the hands of Avaon, the son of Taliesin and Melanghel.

THE END

NOTES

CHAPTER I

1 *Gwen-hudiw*, "the white alluring one:" the name of a mermaid. Used figuratively for the elemental power of the sea.

2 The rapturous and abstracted state of poetical inspiration.

CHAPTER II

3 The accent is on the second syllable: Seithényn.

4 Gwin . . . o eur . . . ANEURIN

5 The mixture of ale and mead made *bradawd*, a favourite drink of the Ancient Britons.

CHAPTER III

7This poem is a specimen of a numerous class of ancient Welsh poems, in which each stanza begins with a repetition of the prominent idea, and terminates with a proverb, more or less apllicable to the subject. In some poems, the sequency of the main images is regular and connected, and the proverbial terminations strictly appropriate: in others, the sequency of the main images is loose and incoherent, and the proverbial termination has little or nothing to do with the subject of the stanza. The basis of the poem in the text is in the *Englynion* of Llwyarch Hên.

8 In the fourteenth and fifteenth books fo the *Dionysiaca* of Nonnus, Bacchus changes the river Astacis into wine; and the multitudinous aremy of water-drinking Indians, proceeding to quench their thirst in the stream, become franticly drunk, and fall an easy prey to the Bacchic invaders. In the thirty-fifth book, ther experiment is repeated on the Hydaspes. *"Ainsi conquesta Bacchus l'Inde,"* as Rabelais has it.

CHAPTER IV

10 Ochenaid Gwyddnau Garanhir

Pan dross y don dros ei dir.

CHAPTER V

11 a small boat of basketwork, sheathed with leather.

12 Mor drist ac Elffin pan gavod Taliesin.

CHAPTER VI

16 Snowdon.

CHAPTER IX

20 This poem has little or nothing of Taliesin's *Canu y Gwynt*, with the exception of the title. That poem is apparently a fragment; and, as it now stands, is an incoherent and scarcely intelligent rhapsody. It contains no distinct or explicit idea, except the proposition that is an unsafe booty to carry off fat kine, which may be easily conceded in a case where nimbleness of heel, both in man and beast, must have been of great importance. The idea from which, if from any thing in the existing portion of the poem, it takes its name, that the whispers of the wind bring rumours of war from Deheubarth, is rather implied than expressed.

21 The spider weaving in suspended armour, is an old emblem of peace and inaction. Thus Bacchylides, in his fragment on Peace:

> *En de sidarodetois porpaxin*
> *Aithan arachnan erga pelontai.*

Euripides, in a fragment of *Erechtheus*:

> *Keisthó doru moi miton amphiplekein*

Arachnais.

And Nonnus, whom no poetical image escaped: (*Dionysiaca*, L. xxxviii.)

> *Ou phonos, ou tote déris; ekeito de télothi charmés*
> *Bakchias hexaetéros arachnioósa boein.*

And Beaumont and Fletcher, in the *Wife for a Month*:

> "Would'st thou live so long, till thy sword hung by,
>   And lazy spiders filled the hilt with cobwebs?"

A Persian poet says, describing ruins:

> "The spider spreads the veil in the palace of the Caesars."

And among the most felicitous uses of this emblem, must never be forgotten Hogarth's cobweb over the lid of the charity-box.

CHAPTER XII

23 Caerlon on Usk, in Wales: London in England: and York in Deira and Bernicia.

25 Mor llawen ag Ngdolig yn Nghaerlleon.

CHAPTER XIV

28 According to the British Chronicles, Brutus, the great grandson of Aeneas, having killed his father, Silvius, to fulfill a prophecy, went to Greece, where he found the posterity of Helenus, the son of Priam; collected all the Trojan race within the limits of Greece; and, after some adventures by land and sea, settled them in Britain, which was before uninhabited, "except for a few giants."

29 Gwrtheryn: Vortigern.

30 Hengist and Horsa.

31 Gwythevyr: Vortimer.

32 Vortigern, who was, on the the death of his son Vortimer, restored to the throne from which he had been deposed.

33 Ronwen: Rowena.

34 Hengist.

35Eidiol or Emrys: Emrys Wledig: Amrosius.

36 Vortigern and Rowena.

37 Hengist.

Lightning Source UK Ltd.
Milton Keynes UK
UKOW050447021111

181318UK00004B/75/P